ISABELLE
Shows Her Stuff

ISABELLE
Shows Her Stuff

Constance C. Greene

A YEARLING BOOK

Published by
Dell Publishing Co., Inc.
1 Dag Hammarskjold Plaza
New York, New York 10017

Yearling ® TM 913705, Dell Publishing Co., Inc.

ISBN: 0-440-44152-8

Reprinted by arrangement with Viking Penguin Inc.

Printed in the United States of America

April 1986

10 9 8 7 6 5 4 3 2 1

CW

For Nora

Chapter One

The day Guy Gibbs moved to Hot Water Street was the best day of his life. How could he miss getting into hot water now? What a stroke of luck! What a neat house! What a neat street!

The house, tall and thin and graying, leaned a little into the wind. There was a birdbath in back, a huge old maple tree in front with a vacant bird's nest swinging from its branches, and a path to the front door made of big round stones that reminded Guy of oversized hopscotch potsies.

All in all, that house was just about perfect.

Living on Hot Water Street was going to change Guy's life. He was sure of that. His heart swelled with excitement as he thought of himself marching down to the principal's office.

"Not *you* again!" the principal would exclaim, clutching his head. "What have you done now?"

Guy hugged himself with delight as he imagined himself pulling up to his house in a police car, the street lined with kids watching, mouths open wide in astonishment. He'd been caught snitching apples. Or pumpkins. Or for shooting out streetlights with a BB gun. Which he didn't have. The important thing was, he'd been caught.

No more goody-goody Guy. That was behind him now. From here on in, he, Guy Gibbs, was on a high roll.

The movers were messing around, trying to figure out how to get the piano into the house without bending it, when a girl wearing a red hat with a ripply brim and carrying a newspaper bag on her shoulder came up the path.

She and Guy stood watching.

"A little to the left, Len!" the head mover hollered. "Easy, now, don't break nothing."

Back and forth they went, trying this way and that.

"You might have to take the legs off," the girl said at last.

The head mover was hot and tired and ready to call

it quits. "Cool it, girlie," he said. "I been in this business twice as long as you been alive. I know what I'm doing. I don't need no upstart kid telling me my own business."

"How long have you been in this business?" the girl asked.

The man yanked a gray handkerchief out of his pocket and wiped his forehead. He cleared his throat and said in a very raspy voice, "How long you been around, toots?"

"I asked you first," she said.

He cleared his throat a second time and, turning his head to one side, sent a glittering ball of spit onto the grass. Then he turned his back on the girl and shouted, "Let's try it another way, Len, see how that works."

"How about if you leave the piano outside and when somebody feels like playing, they can open the window and stick their hands out and play from the inside?"

The mover's thick chest moved mightily as he took a deep breath. His little helper, Len, watched anxiously. Guy kept quiet, waiting for the next move.

"That way," the girl explained, "even if it was winter, even if there was a blizzard, they could put on gloves, wipe off the snow, and still play that old piano."

"It's not old, it's new," said Guy. From far away, a dog barked. Trucks rolled on the turnpike. Guy swallowed noisily.

No one spoke. Then the head mover said, "You belong here?" jerking his thumb in the direction of Guy's new house.

"Nope, I'm the paper boy," the girl said.

"They don't want no paper right at this minute, girlie." The man spoke slowly, carefully, biting off each word as if it were a piece of tough meat. "Why don't you do us all a big favor and get lost, huh? Take off. Vamoose."

"I was only trying to help." She did a little jig.

"Yeah," Guy chimed in, "you don't hafta get a red nose."

"Right," the girl agreed. "What's that mean?"

"My father says it means you don't hafta get riled up," Guy told her, pleased he knew something she didn't.

"I'm gonna pull that on Herbie," she said. "How about asking your mother if she wants the paper delivered?" She whipped out a pencil and pad from her bag. "Philip'll kill me if I don't write everything down."

"Who's Philip?"

"My brother. It's his route. Well, sort of half mine. I'm subbing for him on account of he sprained his ankle. He's got crutches and everything. You'd think he was the first person who ever had crutches." She sighed. "Boys make such a fuss. He won't even let me try 'em out. And you should see the way my mother waits on him. It's enough to make you puke." She rolled her eyes. "What's your name?"

"Guy," he said. "What's yours?"

"Isabelle. Go ask your mom, will you? I'm in a hurry. Herbie's waiting for me. We're fighting at my house today. He might skin out on me if I'm late."

"Why are you fighting with Herbie? Are you mad at him?" Guy asked. To meet a paper boy like Isabelle his first day in the new house was another sign his luck was changing. He could've talked to her all day.

"Heck, no. We're friends. We just like to fight. We fight every day after school. Go ask, will you? I've got to blast off."

Guy raced inside, and Isabelle, snapping her fingers and whistling, began to dance. The movers stopped to watch.

"Whaddya call that?" the little mover asked, scratching his head.

"It's a dance," she said. "I made it up."

"Loony-bin time," the big mover said. "Get to it, Len. Time's a-wasting."

"You said it," Isabelle agreed.

"She says you can start tomorrow," Guy shouted, racing back.

"Okay." Isabelle was all business. "Name and address, please," she said, pencil poised.

"Guy Gibbs," said Guy.

"Father's name, dodo," she said.

"Peter Gibbs, Twenty-two Hot Water Street," he answered proudly.

"Lucky you. I always wanted to live on this street,"

she said, tucking her pad and pencil into her bag.

"Don't forget what I said about the legs," she hollered to the moving men, and then she was off and running, on her way to fight with Herbie.

"Sonny," the big mover said, "count your lucky stars that kid ain't related to you."

"Right," the little mover agreed.

"But maybe she's got something," he said. "Maybe the legs unscrew or something. Let's give it a try."

The big one gave the little one a black look, and they went back to trying to figure out the best way to get the piano into Twenty-two Hot Water Street.

Chapter Two

Guy hadn't made a lot of important decisions in his short life. Should he have chocolate or vanilla, or should he wear his red shirt or his blue—things like that.

But when he decided to follow Isabelle that first day in his new house, he acted as if he'd been making big, important decisions all the days of his life.

She traveled fast. Guy managed to keep up, but only just. He got a bad pain in his side. He wanted to stop and rest. But he was afraid he might lose her. That wouldn't do. So he kept going. When he was at the end of his rope, his tongue hanging out like a dog who'd been chasing cars or sheep, when his heart was pounding so hard it threatened to pop out of his chest, Isabelle got where she was going.

"Where ya been? I almost left!" he heard someone shout.

Guy hid behind a narrow tree, bulging out from behind it on either side. A baby could've spotted him, but neither Isabelle nor Herbie (for surely this was Herbie) seemed to notice him. He watched Isabelle throw down her newspaper bag, settle her hat firmly on her head, and leap like a tiger upon Herbie. Herbie howled as his head hit the ground. They rolled around in the dirt, exchanging blows. Guy came out from behind the tree and squatted at a respectful distance, watching them, entranced. It was like watching a TV Western, he thought. They weren't wearing high-heeled boots. Or ten-gallon hats. And they weren't even breaking chairs over each other's heads, and there wasn't any shooting. But Herbie and Isabelle were making the same noises the TV cowboys made, grunting, groaning, sending up shouts of rage. And it was all live, real—much more exciting than watching TV.

"No feet!" Isabelle hollered suddenly. "We said no feet!" She had relaxed her grip for a second. That was all Herbie needed. He flipped her over, with the aid of his feet. He was winning.

"How come it's okay if *you* use feet but it's not okay

if I do?" Herbie asked quietly. Herbie always got quiet when he was winning.

Isabelle had big feet and she was proud of them. Her feet came in handy, both for fighting and for running.

"Besides," Herbie explained, "I only used one foot. And that's because you were crushing all the bones in my stomach."

"You don't have bones in your stomach," Isabelle said scornfully. "You've got guts. Gobs and gobs of guts. If you stretched 'em out, those guts of yours would probably reach down to the end of the street and around the block."

Herbie didn't like to hear about guts, his own or anyone else's. Guy didn't either, but he listened anyway.

Slowly, lovingly, Isabelle described Herbie's guts to him. "They're all pink and wobbly," she said. "Like giant worms, miles and miles of giant worms, all pink and wobbly, squiggly and slippery."

Guy's stomach began to do flip-flops. Herbie's must've too, because he jumped up and ran over to the curb and began heaving.

Isabelle, a small smile of triumph on her face, went over to investigate.

"You're a faker, Herb," she said. "You didn't throw up one drop. Not one. Some faker you are."

"Leave me alone," Herbie said crossly. "Maybe you

don't have bones in your stomach, but I sure do in mine. Who's that?"

Guy had blown his cover and was practically breathing down their necks by now.

"He's my new customer on my paper route," Isabelle said.

"Wait'll I tell Philip you called it your route!" Herbie howled.

Isabelle assumed her boxer's stance: knees bent, fists held close to her face. She bobbed in circles around Guy, punching at the air around his head. His eyes, shiny and still as two pebbles at the bottom of a pond, followed her. The rest of him was still.

"How old are you?" Isabelle said, still punching.

"Eight," he said softly.

"I'm ten!" Isabelle crowed. "I'm in fifth grade and doing fine in life. How about you?"

"I'm in third grade," he said.

"So? So?" she said, as if he was trying to start trouble. "Hey, Herb, this kid lives on Hot Water Street."

Herbie hooked his thumbs into the waist of his pants, partly to appear tough, partly to hold them up. His mother bought his pants a size too big to allow for shrinkage in the dryer. Herbie was constantly in danger of losing his pants. He sauntered over to Guy, eyes narrowed, sneering a little.

"You look like a straight shooter, pardner," Herbie said. He wiped his hand on his pants and said, "Shake." Guy shook.

"How about you and me wiping up the floor with her?" Herbie suggested. "Two against one? How about it?"

"Okay, you little twerps!" Isabelle roared, advancing on them, fists ready.

At that very moment a voice cried, "Isabelle! Time!"

"Coming!" Isabelle shouted, still advancing on Guy and Herbie.

"I didn't say anything," Guy said in a quavery voice. For the first time he thought perhaps he should've stayed at home.

"You better go, Iz," Herbie said. "I can tell when your mother means it or if she's only fooling around."

"My mother never fools around," Isabelle said.

"Isabelle! Last call!"

Isabelle took one last lucky swing and decked Herbie. He howled as she took off, her Adidas a blur in the gathering dusk.

"She fights dirty," Herbie said, rubbing his ear. "They don't call her Isabelle the Itch for nothing. She's always punching out people. She didn't really hurt me. I always holler and she stops. I was only pretending. If I holler loud enough, she lays off. See you," and Herbie was gone too, flying low.

It was almost dark.

I hope I don't get lost, Guy thought. I hope no monsters are hiding in the bushes. Excitement crowded him. He had made two new friends—big kids, tough kids. Isabelle the Itch and Herbie.

Noises came from the shadows, but he kept going.
At long last the street sign said Hot Water Street.
He was home.

Chapter Three

"*Where'd they put the piano?*" *Isabelle asked, mashing* her face against the screen door, mouth open, enjoying the slightly bitter taste of metal.

Without moving her chin from its nesting place in her hand, the little girl looked at her and said, "Who're you?"

"The paper boy. Where's the piano?" Isabelle opened the door and, uninvited, eased herself inside.

"You looked like a guppy," the little girl said. "With your mouth open like that. Just like our guppy when I feed him."

"How do you know it's a him? I told the movers they might have to take off the legs if they wanted to get the piano inside. Either that or leave it outside, and when your mother wants to play, she could open the window and play from inside."

"My mother doesn't play the piano," the child said. "I do. I take lessons."

"I can play 'Chopsticks,' " Isabelle said. "What's a little twerp like you doing taking piano lessons?" She opened the refrigerator door absent-mindedly and looked inside. It was amazing what some people kept in refrigerators. She knew a girl whose mother was a writer and kept her manuscripts in the refrigerator, in case the house burned down. That way her manuscripts would be safe.

"My mother says you should never open somebody's refrigerator," the little girl said. "It makes her mad when kids do that."

Isabelle closed the door. There was nothing good in there anyway. "Have you got an ice maker?" she asked. Isabelle's father said they were expensive and unnecessary, but she longed for one. They made such neat noises. Little clinking sounds, like fish coming up for air. Or mice having a party.

"We only moved in yesterday. We haven't got settled yet," the little girl said. "I'm not a little twerp. I'm a child."

"You could've fooled me," said Isabelle.

"What's your name?" the child asked.

14

"Isabelle. What's yours?"

"I'm Becca. I'm six. Do you want to see my chains?"

"Sure. Are they gold?"

"No, silly." Becca got down off her chair. "Come on, I'll show you."

There was nothing Isabelle liked better than inspecting other people's houses. Closets were her specialty, but she also liked cellars, attics, bathrooms, rec rooms, and master bedrooms. So far she'd never seen a master in a master bedroom, but she kept trying. My daughter the real-estate lady, her mother sometimes called her.

"They're in here." Becca opened the door to a small room off the kitchen. "This is our playroom, except when my grandmother comes to visit."

The room was crowded with paper chains. The ceiling was festooned with them and they decorated the walls, moving in a slow dance as the draft from the open door stirred them to action. They hung every which way.

"They're like cobwebs," Isabelle said, brushing the chains away from her face. "How come you've got so many?"

"Every time I read a book," Becca said, "I make a chain. That way, I keep count of how many books I've read."

In spite of herself Isabelle was impressed. "I bet you didn't read this many," she said, starting to count Becca's chains.

"There are forty-three," Becca said. "And I read them all. How many books have you read?"

"Oh," Isabelle said, waving her hands in the air, "I don't have time to read. I've got too many things to do. I play soccer. And tap-dance. And fight and do Philip's paper route. And practice the fifty-yard dash. That's my specialty, the fifty-yard dash."

"Everyone has time to read books," Becca said, unimpressed by Isabelle's busy schedule. "If they want to, that is."

This little squirt sounded like Isabelle's teacher, Mrs. Esposito, or like Isabelle's own mother, for Pete's sake.

"What grade are you in?" Isabelle wanted to know.

"I'm in first," Becca said. "I'm a gifted child."

"Okay," said Isabelle, "say something gifted."

"You're cuckoo!" Becca replied, laughing.

"If you're so gifted, how come you're not in high school already? I read about a thirteen-year-old kid who was so smart he was going to college. What's holding you up?" Isabelle demanded.

"I'm too little to be in high school," Becca said calmly.

"Becca, who are you talking to?" a voice called from upstairs.

"I'm talking to Isabelle, the paper boy," Becca called back. "My mother's up in the attic, unpacking things," she told Isabelle.

"Where's your brother? Did he have to stay after school or something?" Isabelle asked.

"Of course not. Guy never has to stay after school."

"He doesn't?" Isabelle asked, amazed. Staying after school was as natural to her as breathing.

"Guy never gets into trouble," Becca said, leading the way back to the kitchen.

Loud noises from outside interrupted them. Isabelle went to the window. "Looks like he's in it now," she said.

Guy came running up the path. Behind him was a gang of boys, all bigger than he. They were singing and shouting and waving their arms. Guy banged in and slammed the door, standing with his back against it, breathing hard. His sweater was torn and his pants were muddy. Tears made tracks through the dirt on his face.

"They followed me," he said.

Outside, the boys sang, "Goody-goody-goody-goody," imitating a train picking up speed. "Goody-goody Guy, wouldn't hurt a fly!" they sang with enthusiasm.

"I thought it would be different, living on Hot Water Street," Guy said sadly. "But it's no use, it's no use at all."

"I'll get 'em for you!" Isabelle cried, exploding out the door and into the midst of the gang. "Pick on somebody your own size, why don't you!" she shrieked, fists flying, feet churning.

Someone stuck out a foot. Isabelle tripped and fell

to the sidewalk, where she lay, feeling sick to her stomach.

"Izzy, Izzy, tin-lizzy Izzy!" they sang. "Izzy, Izzy is a bear, in her flowered underwear!" They must've picked that up from Chauncey Lapidus, Isabelle thought. He'd made up that verse. "Izzy's in a tizzy!"

Then, in the flick of an eye, they disappeared—as if a gigantic eraser had wiped them off the board. As if a trap door had opened and swallowed them all whole.

From where she lay Isabelle watched as a taxi pulled up and a woman wearing a large black hat got out and paid the driver.

"Who are you, little girl?" the woman asked.

"I'm the paper boy," said Isabelle, for what seemed like the tenth time.

"From my experience," the woman said, "that is not the proper way to deliver newspapers." She reached down a hand to help Isabelle to her feet. Then they both marched up the front path, and the woman opened the door to Guy's new house as if she belonged there.

"Who are you?" Isabelle asked the woman, figuring tit for tat was fair.

"I'm Guy's grandmother. I've come for a visit, to help out until they get settled. They're not expecting me, but I'm sure they'll be glad to see me. I haven't been to visit them in ages."

A woman was standing at the sink bathing Guy's dirty face. "Good heavens, Mother Gibbs!" the woman cried. "I certainly didn't expect to see you!"

Isabelle wanted to stay to see what was going to happen, but her canvas bag still bulged with undelivered papers. She laid one on the table and took off.

Chapter Four

"How's my angel?" Guy's grandmother pursed her lips and pointed them in his direction.

"I'm not your angel," Guy said, backing off. "How long are you staying?"

"I just got here," his grandmother said, sitting in the most comfortable chair and crossing her legs. She looked around.

"No ashtrays?" she said.

"Nobody smokes."

"I do," she announced.

"I knew you weren't an angel," she continued. "I'm a little rusty at being a grandmother. That's the way they're supposed to talk to their grandchildren, isn't it? Give me time." She and Guy stared at one another.

From the kitchen Guy's mother called, "Be right out, Mother Gibbs."

"I wish she wouldn't call me that," Guy's grandmother said. "Makes me feel like an old lady in an apron."

"What should she call you?" Guy asked, thinking she *was* old, even if she didn't wear an apron.

"My name."

"What's your name?"

"Maybelle." She looked pleased. "I was born in May and I was a beautiful baby."

"You were?" Guy said, not believing her. He didn't think a whole lot of Maybelle as a name, but he kept quiet, studying her. He hadn't seen his grandmother since he'd been a tiny baby. At least, that's what they told him. He was pretty sure he could remember her peering down at him and saying, "Skinny little shaver, isn't he?" If it wasn't her, it was somebody just like her.

"Hello," said Becca, appearing in the doorway.

"Who's that?" Guy's grandmother said, squinting through the smoke of the cigarette she'd lit.

"That's my sister, Becca," Guy said.

"Oh, right. I forgot about her. How's it going, Becca?" Guy's grandmother said.

"This is my grandmother, Becca," Guy said.

"She's my grandmother, too, don't forget," Becca said. "Your lungs will turn black if you smoke."

"Who said?" Guy's grandmother asked, raising her eyebrows.

After a short silence Becca said, "I'm a gifted child."

"Who said?" Guy's grandmother asked again.

"Who said what?"

"That you're a gifted child." Guy's grandmother blew out a huge cloud of smoke, and Becca went into a coughing fit.

"I'm in a special class for gifted children," Becca said, when she'd finished her coughing fit.

"And what about you, Guy?" his grandmother asked.

"I'm an underachiever," Guy said in a loud voice. "What's more, they call me goody-goody because I can't get into trouble."

"Everybody in school calls him Goody-Goody Guy," Becca put in her two cents.

Guy clenched his fists and shouted, "Shut up! Who asked you?"

"How about an ashtray?" Guy's grandmother said. Guy raced into the kitchen and returned in the nick of time with an old orange-juice can. They all watched as the ash trembled and fell into the can.

"Here we are, Mother Gibbs," Guy's mother cried, carrying in a tray of refreshments.

"Call her Maybelle, that's her name," Guy said.

"Guy," his mother said sternly, "she's your grandmother."

"How long is she staying?" Becca asked.

"It depends. Maybe a week, maybe a month." Guy's grandmother looked around at them. "Depends on how much you need me."

"A month," Guy's mother said, handing round a plate of little cakes. "How nice."

Guy's grandmother took out another cigarette. "How about a match?" she said.

"I can't stand the smell of smoke," said Becca. "It makes me sick."

"Well, don't go getting a red nose about it." Guy's grandmother put the cigarette back in her handbag.

"I got a copy of *Grimm's Fairy Tales* for being the best reader in my class," Becca said.

"That beats a sharp stick in the eye. Read that," and Guy's grandmother snatched up the newspaper and pointed to the headline.

Becca said, "Oh, I only read books," and twirled out of the room.

Guy's grandmother turned her dark, deep-set eyes on him. He lifted his shoulders as if to say, "What can I do?"

"She's something." Guy's grandmother tapped her fingers on the table, then dove into her handbag and came up with another cigarette. They both looked at it. She put it back in her bag.

"So they call you goody-goody, do they?" she said.

Guy squeezed his hands between his knees and clicked his feet together rhythmically.

"That's not the worst thing in the world," she said.

Guy's feet clicked, lickety split, faster and faster.

"I'm glad I came," Guy's grandmother said.

Chapter Five

If my name was Jake, things would be different.

Guy stared at himself in the mirror.

If my name was Jake, they would never chase a person named Jake, hollering "Goody-goody Jake!" It would never happen. A person named Jake wouldn't take any guff from anybody. "Everything's jake," his father said when he meant everything was fine and dandy. Catch him saying "Everything's Guy." Just catch him.

Guy lifted his lip and sneered at himself. Jake

sounded tough. Already he looked different. Mean. Tough. Beware of Jake, they'd whisper. Don't rub Jake the wrong way. You know Jake. He'll take off your ear in one bite.

He turned sideways and sneered some more. He reminded himself of a pro football player he'd seen on TV. Yup, he was definitely a Jake. The thought cheered him as he put on his socks and sneaks. Then the jeans. Oops. He always forgot. The jeans wouldn't go over the sneaks. Off with the sneaks, on with the jeans.

The minute he woke up that morning Guy had smelled Saturday—crispy, spicy, fragrant, as if his mother had taken a freshly baked apple pie from the oven. He planned to spend today with Isabelle, only she didn't know it. He'd better hot-foot it over to her house before she and Herbie went somewhere.

Guy wet his hands and smashed down his cowlick. People named Jake who were mean and tough didn't have cowlicks on the top of their heads. But in its own way, the cowlick was mean and tough, too. It sprang back up like a jack-in-the-box.

On weekdays, Guy dawdled. On Saturdays, he dressed with the speed of a volunteer fireman. Down the stairs he went, two at a time.

"For a little boy," his mother said in her soft voice, "you make a great deal of noise. Cereal's ready."

"I'm not eating cereal," Guy said in a loud, rude

voice. "I don't have time for cereal," Guy/Jake said. "I gotta get going."

"Have to, not gotta," said his mother gently. Everything she said and did was gentle.

"Too bad," she told him. "The cinnamon doughnuts are almost warm."

He *knew* he'd smelled Saturday. He ate his cereal fast, wishing, not for the first time, for a dog. A dog would sure love that bowl of cereal, Guy thought. A dog would be company, would lick his hand, and would sleep at the foot of his bed at night. A dog would guard the house. A dog would be a friend. But a dog was messy and a lot of trouble. And expensive—to feed, to take to the vet's.

"Guy," his mother said. He almost said "My name's Jake," but didn't. "Guy, if those boys bother you again, I want you to promise to tell me. I'll do something about it. That's not right. Dad wouldn't like it either." They tried never to bother Dad with tales of Guy being teased. Dad didn't like to hear this—he liked to think Guy was an all-around-American-boy-type who was never called names and made fun of. Guy's father was the football coach at the high school. He planned on Guy being a football player someday. Being a football player was way down at the end of Guy's list of favorite things to think about.

"I'm done." Guy showed his mother the bottom of his dish. The doughnut was his. Cradling it in his hand, he headed for the door.

"I'm going to Isabelle's," he told her.

"Who is Isabelle?"

"The paper boy. She was here yesterday "

"She called me a twerp," Becca said.

"You are," said Guy.

"Guy," his mother said, "that's not nice."

"Isabelle asked me over to her house today." Guy looked at his mother from under lowered lids. He almost never lied, and he was surprised when she seemed to believe what he said. "Isn't Isabelle a trifle too old for you to play with?" was all she said.

"She's only ten," he said. *Only* ten! She was practically a teenager, that's what. He didn't tell his mother about Isabelle and Herbie fighting every day after school. She wouldn't like that, he knew.

"Don't wear out your welcome," his mother told him as he said good-bye.

When he got to Isabelle's, there was no answer to his knock. Guy sat on the back step to wait. Presently the door opened and a man carrying a bag of garbage almost fell over him.

"Oops!" said the man. "Sorry, didn't see you."

"Is Isabelle up yet?" Guy asked.

"No, thank God," the man said. "I have the place all to myself. If you promise to be quiet, not say a word, you can come in and wait."

"I promise," Guy said.

Once in, the man pointed a floury finger and said,

"Sit there. And remember, no talking. I can't cook and talk at the same time."

Guy sat. The man whistled happily, sifting flour, checking a cookbook spread open on the counter. "I think I've got it!" he cried out once or twice. "I really think I've got it! It's not easy, making pizza from scratch," he told Guy. "And it's not cheap either. Cheese, sausages, anchovies, all that stuff. But the real trick is the dough. That's the tough part. You have to be quick when you toss it up and catch it. You ever seen 'em throw it up in the air in a pizza store, then catch it on its way down?" Guy shook his head no. "Fantastic! Absolutely fantastic!" the man said. "They never miss. Toss it up, twirl it around, then toss it up again. I wish I could do it. I'm learning, though. Don't want to rush it. Easy does it, eh?"

Guy nodded, smiling. He was enjoying the conversation, even if he hadn't said a word.

Isabelle zoomed into the kitchen and headed straight for the refrigerator. "Hi," she said to Guy, not at all surprised to see him there. "Dad," she said to the pizza man, "I've decided to leave my body to science."

"That so?" Isabelle's father leaned over his cookbook, muttering to himself. A large boy on crutches appeared. Philip, Guy figured, as clever as any detective. That's Philip.

"I'm leaving my body to science," Isabelle told Philip.

"Suppose they give it back?" Philip speared a pickle

from a jar. "What do they want with a wimpy little bod like yours?"

Isabelle gave it one more try. "I'm leaving my body to science," she told Guy in a loud voice, as if she thought he might be deaf.

Guy nodded to show he'd heard and then laid a finger against his lips.

"Who's he?" Philip aimed a crutch in Guy's direction. "Where'd he come from?"

"He's a new customer on my . . . I mean, your paper route. Better treat him nice or he might cancel. His name's Guy," said Isabelle.

Guy opened his mouth to say his name was Jake, then remembered his promise to keep quiet.

"What's your prob, kid? Cat got your tongue?" Philip asked.

Isabelle's father ran his hand through his hair, leaving white tracks. "I've been at this since dawn and I'm still a long way from finishing. You can talk now," he told Guy. "I'm tired of making bread," he said to them. "I'm letting my imagination soar and making pizza instead."

"Go for it, Dad," Philip said.

"My father always makes bread on Saturday," Isabelle explained. "I take a loaf to my teacher. She's on a diet, but she eats my father's bread anyway because it's so delicious."

Guy, who had been wondering what to say now that he no longer had to be silent, said, "My father gave blood once. After, they gave him a glass of orange juice. And my grandmother said she might donate her organs."

Then he tapped his feet and stared at the ceiling, having talked himself out.

"Cool," Isabelle said. "I wouldn't mind donating my organs."

"Which organ did you have in mind?" Isabelle's father asked, pausing in his pizza-making.

"Which one do you think would be best?" Isabelle asked, not having the faintest idea what organs were.

"How about your brain?" Philip suggested. "If you donated your brain to science, they could give it to a monkey and that old monkey would be the smartest monkey on his block."

"Har-de-har," Isabelle said.

"The brain isn't an organ," Isabelle's father said, kneading his dough. Isabelle pointed a finger at Philip, laughing hugely and silently at his mistake.

"Make it your liver or your kidneys," Isabelle's father said.

"Liver and kidneys!" Isabelle made throw-up noises. Then, as if she'd just made it up, she did an elaborate dance, crooning "excellent, excellent" to herself, praising her own talents.

"I'm off to Angelo's now. Hands off my dough. Your mother's still asleep, so keep the noise down, please. Angelo's giving me a lesson in how to toss the dough up and catch it coming down. I'll be back in an hour."

The telephone rang and Isabelle raced to answer. Philip gave her a hip check and sent her crashing against the wall.

"Hello," their father said. "No, I'm sorry. They're both busy misbehaving. Call back, please." He hung up. "Shape up or ship out," he said. "You both behave like troglodytes."

"What's that?" Isabelle asked.

"Cave men. And they didn't have telephones."

"Who was it?" asked Philip.

"I didn't ask. The young lady didn't leave her name."

"I knew it was for me!" Philip howled.

"I bet it was Mary Eliza Shook. She always checks up on me on Saturday."

"Remember what I said. Hands off the dough." They listened as their father started the car and drove away.

"Turkey," Philip said.

"I'm telling Dad you called him a turkey!" Isabelle cried.

"Not him, scuzz. You."

"Dinosaur breath," said Isabelle.

Guy scrooched down in his chair and folded his hands on his stomach, like an old man taking the sun on a park bench, enjoying himself.

Disgusted, Philip crutched his way out, muttering "spoiled brat" and "stink baby" and other endearments.

Isabelle took a can of Reddi Wip from the refrigerator and shot some into her mouth.

"Open," she said to Guy, like a dentist. He opened and she shot some into his mouth.

"It's sweet," Guy said, surprised.

"What'd you expect, sour?" Isabelle took something out of a drawer and pulled it on over her head.

"What's that?"

"It's my mother's old pantyhose. I'm trying it out on Herbie's mother. I like to freak her out. Robbers wear pantyhose masks when they don't want people to know who they are. I bet Herbie's mother won't know who I am. Maybe she'll think I'm a robber. That oughta really get her," she announced with satisfaction.

"It makes your voice sound funny," said Guy. "And it makes you look funny, too."

"Good." Isabelle lifted the cloth her father had placed over his pizza dough and poked it with one finger. "I'm just testing to see if anything's happened yet," she said.

"You father said hands off," Guy reminded her.

"I only touched it a tiny bit. He won't know. Not unless you tell him," she said, scowling at Guy.

"Cross my heart," he said. "I won't tell."

"All right," she said. "Let's go."

Chapter Six

"*Herbie can't come out today. He's got a cold.*" *Herbie's* mother looked straight at Isabelle and didn't scream once. Not even a tiny little scream.

"He didn't have one yesterday," Isabelle said indignantly, from behind her pantyhose mask.

"Well, he has one today." Herbie's mother opened the door a fraction and said to Guy, "What's your name?"

"Guy," said Isabelle.

"Jake," said Guy.

Herbie's mother looked surprised. "You kids better get your act together," she said.

"Don't you notice anything?" Isabelle slowly turned her head from left to right, right to left.

Herbie's mother narrowed her eyes and studied Isabelle carefully. "Now that you mention it," she said, "I *did* think you were Mary Eliza Shook for a minute."

Isabelle crossed her eyes and tried to stick her thumbs in her ears and waggle her fingers to show how she felt about looking like Mary Eliza Shook, but the pantyhose got in the way.

"But when I heard your voice," Herbie's mother said, smiling, "I knew it was you."

"Let 'em in, Mom!" Isabelle heard Herbie shout. She looked through the door and saw Herbie teetering on the top step. He had on his astronaut pajamas and his crash helmet. He didn't look the least bit sick.

Herbie's mother turned her head and shouted, "Get back to bed!" And in a flash Isabelle thrust the toe of her Adidas in the crack in the door, an opening wedge.

"Hey, Herb!" she cried, her mouth against the crack. "How about a game of Crazy Eights or Monopoly?"

Isabelle and Herbie hadn't played Monopoly since the time when she'd made some counterfeit money and tried to pass it off as the real Monopoly stuff. Herbie was still sore about that.

"Sorry." Herbie's mother almost shut Isabelle's nose in the door. "Herbie's off-limits today. He had a temperature last night." She shut the door firmly in their faces.

"Maybe it's catching!" Isabelle cried. "Let us in! It might be catching!"

But Herbie's mother slid the lock into place and waved good-bye to them. "Boy," said Isabelle, "I bet Herbie's drinking orange juice by the quart today. His mother feeds him vitamin C to keep him from getting colds. He gets colds anyhow. Let's wait out front. Herbie'll come and talk to us out the window. Come on."

Guy hadn't said a single word except "Jake" when asked what his name was. "I changed my name to Jake," he told Isabelle.

"When?"

"Yesterday. I figure if my name's Jake, it'll make me tougher, and they won't call me goody-goody Jake, that's for sure."

"Maybe." Isabelle looked doubtful. "Don't put any money on it, though. There he is! Hey, Herb," she called.

Herbie opened the upstairs window and leaned out. "What's that on your head?" he croaked.

"My mother's pantyhose. It's a mask like the ones robbers wear when they rob a bank. So nobody'll recognize 'em. Your mother knew who I was right away, though. By my voice, she said," Isabelle told Herbie.

"If you rob a bank," Herbie said, "you write a note and shove it to the person you're robbing. That way you don't have to talk and give it all away." He coughed loudly to prove he was sick.

"Send some germs down to us," Isabelle called up. "Me and Guy could use a few germs."

Herbie opened the window further and breathed out a lot of germs.

"Too bad you can't come with us," Isabelle said. "My father's making pizza today. I have to go home and help him throw the dough up in the air."

"What kind's he making?" Herbie said.

"Onion and pepperoni," she said. It was Herbie's favorite kind.

"Ooh!" Herbie wailed. His mother came up behind him and slammed the window down. Herbie disappeared.

"Let's put the show on the road," Isabelle said, whipping off her mask and stuffing it in her pocket.

Mary Eliza Shook materialized as if she'd been waiting for them. She wore her jogging suit, a sweatband, and leg warmers.

Isabelle made a face. "Your legs are all wrinkly," she said.

Mary Eliza looked at her legs with great fondness. "Those are leg warmers," she said. "All ballet dancers wear them. Other people wear them too, but they're not professionals. Only ballet dancers should really wear leg warmers. If their legs get cold, they might get cramps."

"Then what?" Isabelle said.

"Then they can't dance, dummy." Mary Eliza's arms arched over her head as she prepared her next *pas de chat.*

"Plenty of people wear leg warmers and they're not ballet dancers," Isabelle told Mary Eliza. "My brother Philip says girls who wear 'em have elephant legs. That's what he calls 'em, Elephant Legs, because they make your legs look all wrinkly, like an elephant's. Who needs it?"

"Who's the boyfriend, dear? Aren't you robbing the cradle?" Mary Eliza let out a blast of her most irritating laughter. Isabelle silenced her with a direct hit from her ring.

"Cut it out," Mary Eliza said. "If he's not your boyfriend, who is he?"

A line from a TV movie she'd recently seen popped into Isabelle's head.

"He's me little brudder, that's who," she said. Guy's mouth dropped open in astonishment as she laid a protective arm on his shoulder. He flinched, thinking she was going to belt him.

"Pooh!" said Mary Eliza. "You don't have a little brother and you know it."

"We just adopted him," said Isabelle, getting a firmer grip on Guy. All of a sudden, the idea of a little brother was very attractive. She could boss him around and everything. A little brother, Isabelle suddenly decided, beat a big brother all hollow.

"What's his name, Miss Smarty?"

"His name's Jake. Say hello to the lady, Jake." Isabelle dug her elbow into Guy's ribs.

"Hello," said Guy, dipping his head and staring at the sidewalk, trying to work free of Isabelle's clinging hands. In case she was going to nudge him again, he'd rather be far away from her.

"Well, all I can say is, it's very strange, very strange indeed," Mary Eliza muttered. She darted at Isabelle, ready to link arms, a terrible habit of hers. But Isabelle was too fast for her. She stuck out her fist with the point of her friendship ring aimed straight for Mary Eliza's nose. That did it. Mary Eliza backed off. But she didn't take defeat lightly.

"All right, then!" she shouted. Words failed her.

"You shout too much," Guy said.

"She sure does!" Mary Eliza said, at the top of her voice.

"Not her, you," said Guy. "You make me tired, you shout so much."

"Let's go get some of Dad's homemade pizza," Isabelle said. "I'm hungry, Jake. How about you?" They left Mary Eliza doing a perfect *entrechat* for anyone passing by to see.

"Thanks for calling me Jake," Guy said.

"That's okay. Anytime," said Isabelle, filled with a glow of well-being.

Which didn't last long, for the minute she saw her father's face, she knew he'd discovered her fingerprint in the pizza dough.

"You just can't keep your hands off, can you?" he said. "I ought to put you over my knee and give you an old-fashioned spanking. That's what you deserve. I should've known better than to leave it within your reach." He swatted her with his rolling pin. It wasn't a very hard swat, but it left flour on her rear end.

Isabelle's mother, washing her hair at the kitchen sink, peered up at her and asked, "Who's that?" meaning Guy.

"He's me little brudder," Isabelle said, fooling around.

"What did you say?" her mother asked, through her dripping hair.

"He's Guy from my paper route, Mom." Isabelle didn't want to push either of her parents any further today. "I brought him home for a piece of Dad's pizza."

"The pizza won't be much good," her father said. "The crust's ruined. When I said 'hands off' I meant exactly that. But Angelo gave me a lesson in throwing the dough up and catching it, so I'm going to go ahead."

The telephone rang. "That's for me," Isabelle's father said. "I'm expecting a call." He wiped his hands on his pants and went into the hall to answer the phone. Isabelle looked at the large circle of dough lying on the counter. Isabelle's mother wrapped a towel around her head and disappeared. The kitchen was very still. Isabelle listened to her father talking on the telephone.

It would be so easy, she thought. Toss it up, catch

it coming down. She'd watched Angelo plenty of times. The way he did it, it looked like a snap.

"Oh, no," Guy said very softly, as she scooped up her father's dough from the counter and held it in both hands.

With a flourish, Isabelle flipped it up into the air. She and Guy watched it go, circling lazily overhead, moving slowly, like a miniature flying saucer. Perfect. Absolutely perfect.

Things got out of control. The circle of dough descended much faster than it had risen. Swift as a falling star, it came down to earth and landed smack on Isabelle's head.

Guy put his hand over his mouth to hold back his giggles. "You look so funny!" he said. Isabelle's father stood in the doorway. Isabelle's mother came downstairs. Silently, she handed Isabelle a hand mirror.

She did indeed look funny. The dough hung limply around her ears, covering her hair and most of her face.

"Tell you what, Isabelle." She heard her father's voice, although she couldn't see him through the curtain of dough. "We'll make the pizza anyway. Just gather it together off your head and roll it out again. It'll be terrible, probably very tough, but it's the best you're going to get today. And you know what?"

"No, sir," Isabelle said.

She could hear her father smiling.

"You get the piece with the most hair in it," he said.

Chapter Seven

Guy sped toward home. After they'd eaten the pizza, which turned out to be not bad after all, he'd helped Isabelle deliver papers. An old lady named Mrs. Stern wasn't home, which disappointed Guy. Isabelle had told him Mrs. Stern painted her front door, as well as the rooms of her house, a different color any time she felt like it—sometimes just to cheer herself up. Guy liked that idea and thought about painting his room dark blue so he could paste some stars on the walls and ceiling. Then he could lie in bed and see the stars shining above and around him and pretend he was camping out.

The wind was rising, making whispery noises in the trees. "Tell your mother I'll collect next week," Isabelle had said. "I'm hoping Philip will still be on crutches. Then she smiled and added, "If his hurt ankle gets better, I can always put a skate at the top of the stairs, and he might fall over it and hurt his other ankle. We'll see." She would, too, Guy thought, full of admiration. Even if Philip was a teenager, Isabelle could handle him. She was awesome.

The sky was smeared with scarlet and gold and looked, Guy thought, like a finger painting he'd done last year. It was his favorite and still hung above his bed. When he grew up, he was going to be an artist. He'd seen paintings done by grown-up artists that looked like finger paintings and which had been sold for a lot of money too. If they could do it, why couldn't he?

The dark clumps of bushes took on the shape of people. "Here he comes," the wind whispered. "Here he comes," they sighed.

Here who comes?

A small, dark shape rushed out at him, and Guy let out a little shout of fear.

"Oh," he said, drawing a deep breath when he saw the little brown dog. "It's only you." He knelt down and patted the dog's soft fur. The dog licked Guy's hand with his rough tongue, and they became immediate friends.

"You're just the right size," Guy told the dog, who wriggled with pleasure. "You could come home with me if my mother would let you," Guy said. "She might let you stay. I'm not sure. If you're good. If you don't go to the bathroom on the rug. Or chew the furniture. Or eat a lot. A dog is a big responsibility, you know." The dog tilted its head to one side and considered this information. It was a frisky little dog, with a tail like a feather duster and eager amber eyes. It would be a good dog to play Frisbee with, Guy thought. It would be a good watchdog, even though it was small, because it could be fierce when fierceness was needed.

"I could hide you in the attic," Guy said aloud. "Keep you a secret until I talked her into loving you. Why don't we try it?" The more he thought about hiding the dog in the attic, the better the idea seemed.

The dog laid a stick at Guy's feet and backed off, barking. So Guy threw the stick and the little dog brought it back, triumphant. Guy threw the stick a second time and the dog went after it again. Guy heard him barking but he didn't return. Guy called and called—"Hey, I'm over here!"—but still the dog didn't appear.

"All right for you!" Guy shouted at last, when he could hardly see the outline of the trees, it was getting so dark. He scurried homeward, turning now and then,

44

checking to see if the dog was following him. But he was alone.

"It's late, Guy," his mother said. "You should have been home long ago. I was very worried."

"I had to help Isabelle deliver her papers," he said. "Here's ours," and he handed over the paper.

"She called," his mother said.

"Isabelle?" he asked, surprised.

"She said for you to come over tomorrow. She said she and Herbie are probably going to fight and you could watch. What's that all about?"

"Oh, they fight all the time. They're friends but they just like to fight," he said, making it sound perfectly normal to like to fight.

"I don't want you fighting, Guy," she said. "You might get hurt."

"I don't know how to fight," he said, and went up to his room and lay on his bed, looking at the ceiling, trying to imagine how it would look pasted all over with stars. His mother found him there.

"I would like to paint my room dark blue and paste stars on it so it would be like the night," he told her.

"Guy." She laid an anxious hand on his forehead. "Do you feel all right?"

"I feel fine," he said, bounding up and down to prove he felt fine. "I just want to paint my room dark blue to cheer myself up. That's all."

Chapter Eight

"Aunt Maude, this is my friend Guy," Isabelle said.

"How do you do? I'm happy to meet you," said Aunt Maude, who had stopped in after church, as usual, to show off her new hat. Guy said hello. Aunt Maude turned to Isabelle's mother and said in a loud whisper, "Hasn't he shrunk?"

"Shrunk?"

"Yes. The little boy, I mean. He seems to have gotten smaller."

"Oh, you've got him confused with Herbie, Maude.

This is a different boy. His family has just moved into a house on Hot Water Street."

"Oh, my." Aunt Maude's eyes rolled, and she said, "I've always thought that would be a very hazardous place to live. All that water boiling around, don't you know." Aunt Maude settled herself on the couch like a hen on its nest.

"My hair seems to be getting thin," she said, patting her freshly washed, newly blonde coiffure.

"Who wants fat hair?" Isabelle said, poking Guy and avoiding her mother's eye, knowing it would be shooting daggers at her.

Fortunately, Aunt Maude's hearing wasn't what it had once been. "I'll take a bald man any day," she continued, "but I do think there's something rather unattractive about a bald woman, don't you agree?"

Isabelle's mother murmured something about having to see to dinner. On her way out she stepped over Isabelle, who was lying on the floor, reading the comics. "Watch it," she said, putting her foot in the middle of Isabelle's back.

"What smells so good?" Aunt Maude sniffed the air delicately.

"Roast pork," Isabelle's mother called out.

"Nobody noticed my hat," Aunt Maude said, getting up and revolving slowly, showing off her hat from every angle. It was made of pale felt and had a wide brim.

"Where on earth did you get it?" Isabelle's mother said, coming back into the room.

"At a tag sale. I don't know what I did before someone invented tag sales. They are a marvel. Absolutely a marvel. There's nothing you can't find at a tag sale."

"If only you had a black mask," Isabelle told Aunt Maude, "you'd look like the Lone Ranger."

"My stars! The Lone Ranger! I haven't heard anyone mention him in donkey's years. Where'd you hear about him?"

"My friend Mrs. Stern told me about him and his horse Silver. They were always doing good deeds, she said. She used to listen to them on the radio. She showed me a picture of him and his friend Tonto. After the Lone Ranger did a good deed, he hollered, 'Hi yo, Silver, away!' and you heard the sound of galloping hooves."

"Sounds like a drag to me," said Philip, in his super bored voice.

"Then a voice said, 'Who *was* that masked man?' like he was the Incredible Hulk or something," Isabelle went on, "and a voice said, 'That was the Lone Ranger.'"

"And Tonto called the Lone Ranger 'Kemosabe,'" Aunt Maude put in. "I remember that much, although of course I was very young at the time." She gently patted her thin hair.

"El Wimpo Kemosabe," Philip said under his breath.

"I always say roast pork isn't roast pork without

48

applesauce," said Aunt Maude, getting back to the matter at hand. "Are you having applesauce?"

"If it isn't roast pork, what is it?" Philip asked Isabelle. Philip got away with murder around Aunt Maude. Never having had any children of her own, she was partial to boys.

"Of course, darling, we're having applesauce. I've set a place for you—I hope you'll stay."

"Oh, I couldn't possibly!" Aunt Maude cried. They went through this every Sunday. She always stayed.

"Would you like to stay for dinner, Guy? We've plenty of everything," Isabelle's mother said.

"I've already aten," Guy said. "Eaten, I mean." He blushed furiously, embarrassed at having mixed up his words. He hadn't eaten dinner, he was just too shy to say he'd like to stay. Plus, he was a very picky eater, and he couldn't remember whether he liked roast pork or not.

"Why," Guy said, really looking at Aunt Maude for the first time, "you look just like my uncle!"

"How so?" she said in a somewhat haughty manner, not at all sure she liked being told she looked like Guy's uncle.

"He's a state trooper," Guy said, "and he has a hat just like yours. Plus, he carries a gun."

Aunt Maude gave a little scream of pleasure at this interesting information. "Perhaps this is a state trooper's hat and I didn't even know it," she said, running her hand over her hat's brim.

When dinner was announced, Guy sat with the family, even though he wasn't hungry. The roast pork certainly smelled good. Maybe he'd never had any. Suddenly, he was starving. But he didn't have the nerve to say he'd changed his mind.

As if he knew what Guy was thinking, Isabelle's father said, "Send this down to the young man from Hot Water Street," slicing off some pork and putting it on a plate. Guy ate it in one gulp. It was delicious. He folded his hands in his lap and kept an eye on the other plates. "Help yourself to applesauce and pass it down," Isabelle whispered, giving him an elbow in the ribs. Then the corn pudding was passed, and Guy had a spot of that. All in all, he did pretty well, especially for someone who'd already eaten.

Aunt Maude asked Philip what he was up to these days. When his ankle was better, that is.

"Well, I'm on the Y swim team," Philip said. "I'm a Webfoot. I do the butterfly in record time. I won a race last month. Next month I swim against the state champs."

Each time Philip said "I" Isabelle counted, mouthing the numbers "One, two, three, four, five" so everyone would know Philip had said "I" five times.

"Isabelle, we can do without that," her mother said. When dinner was over, Isabelle's father said, "Why don't you repair to the parlor, Maude, and put your feet up and rest so we can clear the table."

Aunt Maude always got out of KP duty because she

broke things. When Isabelle caught on to this, she broke a plate (old) and a cup (new) the next time she was called upon to clear. All she got was yelled at.

"You take out the salt and pepper," Isabelle told Guy. "You didn't eat much so you don't have to do much."

"I ate quite a lot. I had two pieces of meat and some applesauce and—"

"Just do what I say, and when we're finished, I'm going to give you a lesson."

"Doing what?" Guy asked.

"In fighting," Isabelle said.

Guy dropped the salt shaker on the floor. Isabelle picked it up and said, "Lucky for you it didn't break. Wait'll I crumb the table, then we'll head out." Crumbing the table was Isabelle's favorite part of Sunday dinner. With a large napkin and her usual enthusiasm, she brushed all the crumbs that had fallen on the table during the meal into a tray. The floor needed crumbing, too, after she'd finished.

"Okay." She regarded the clean tablecloth with a practiced eye. "Mission accomplished. Let's go."

"Is Herbie still sick?" Guy asked, longing for Herbie to be up-and-at-'em so *he* could fight with Isabelle.

"I called him up this morning," Isabelle said, "and his mother said he was in bed. But I could hear him hollering in the background that he was fine. He called his mother a mean old witch because she wouldn't let him out. If I called my mother a mean old witch, she'd wash my mouth out with soap. Come on," and she dragged Guy behind her as she left.

"Don't go far," her mother said.

"Why not?"

"I don't know," her mother said, surprised. "If I call you, I want you to be able to hear me."

Outside at last, Isabelle said, "Okay, put up your dukes."

"I don't have any dukes," said Guy. "I just remembered—I didn't thank your mother. I better go back in and thank her."

Isabelle grabbed Guy's sweater and wouldn't let go. "You don't have to thank her," she said. "We better get going. Dukes are fists, dummy. You got fists. Make a fist." She showed him how. "That's right. Now hit me. Here." She stuck her chin at him. "Hit me as hard as you can. I can take it."

He swung at her and missed.

"Again!" Isabelle shouted.

Fists flailing, Guy stirred up the air around Isabelle's head, but he never hit her.

"You're not trying," she said, sounding like Mrs. Esposito. "You're not concentrating. How can you fight if you don't try?"

"I don't know," Guy said.

Suddenly, two creeps from the fourth grade came swooping down the street on their bikes. They headed straight for where Isabelle and Guy were standing.

"Guy, schmy, couldn't hurt a fly!" one of the boys

bellowed. Guy darted behind a tree and Isabelle took off after the boys. But as fast as she could run, their bikes were faster. One of them spit at her and the other cackled and called names all the way to the end of the block and around the corner until they were out of sight.

When she came back, panting and out of breath, Guy was still behind the tree, waiting for her.

"I don't know what we're gonna do," she said. "You don't want to fight. You can't get into trouble. It's hopeless."

He nodded. "I know," he said. "I thought you could help me."

"I'll think of something," Isabelle said. "But it won't be easy. You're a tough case. I'll need a couple of days. But I'll think of something."

Chapter Nine

The next morning Guy pounced on Isabelle as she came out of her classroom.

"Did you think of anything yet?" he said.

"Give me a break. That was only yesterday," she told him.

"Isabelle, may I see you for a minute, please?" Mrs. Esposito said from the doorway.

"Uh-oh." Isabelle knew that meant trouble.

"Look at this." Mrs. Esposito waved a paper marked with a large red F in Isabelle's face. "Last week's test.

Multiplication tables, the ones I drilled you in. The ones I told you we'd have on the test. There's no excuse for the number you had wrong. Absolutely no excuse. You don't concentrate. You don't pay attention. Your mind is always someplace else. I want to help, Isabelle." Mrs. Esposito's pretty eyes were troubled. "But I can't do it without your cooperation."

If Mrs. Esposito felt bad about Isabelle's F, Isabelle felt worse. Already she could hear her father saying, "Pull yourself together, Isabelle, or we lower the boom." Lowering the boom meant no television, no fun, no nothing. She could see her mother's disappointed face as she said, "I thought you were going to do better."

Isabelle spent a lot of time trying to do better, but it was like running in place. She never got anywhere.

And worst of all, she could hear Philip singing under his breath, singing songs about Scuzzy Izzy. And worse.

"I tried," Isabelle said, jigging first on one foot, then the other. "I really tried."

"No, Isabelle, I don't think you did. If you had, this wouldn't have happened. What am I going to do with you?"

"I know." Isabelle snapped her fingers, delighted with the idea that had just occurred to her. "I could come home with you and stay at your house a while. A week or a month, maybe. Then you could drill me on my multiplication tables every morning before school. How would that be?" Isabelle had never been to Mrs. Esposito's house and had always wanted to see what it was like.

Mrs. Esposito shuddered slightly. "No," she said, "I'm sure your mother and father would never permit that."

"They might," Isabelle said. "They get fed up with me. Maybe if I went to live with you, they'd be sorry they were so mean to me."

"I'm sure your mother and father aren't mean to you, Isabelle."

"Oh, yes, they are. They say I'm a pest and a terrible itch and they make me go to my room until I simmer down. My mother says I'm making her old before her time, and my brother kicks me in the stomach when they're out and locks me in the bathroom and steals my candy. Even when I hide it in my shoes, he finds it and eats it. He says it smells of feet but he eats it anyway."

Mrs. Esposito laughed. "One thing about you, Isabelle, you always cheer me up. Even when I'm cross with you, you cheer me up."

"That's good." Isabelle danced around Mrs. Esposito. "My father made pizza Saturday. The crust was a little tough but he said to tell you next time it'll be better and you can have some."

"Tell your father I'd like that." Mrs. Esposito handed Isabelle her test paper. "Take this home," she said, "and go over it. Correct all the mistakes you made and bring it back tomorrow."

"Do I have to have my mother or father sign it?" Isabelle asked.

Mrs. Esposito sighed. "Not this time. This will be between you and me. Just this once."

Isabelle threw her arms around Mrs. Esposito and almost knocked her down. "I love you!" she cried. "You're the most excellent teacher in the whole world!"

She raced out of the room and almost bumped into Jane Malone.

"Sally Smith is moving," Jane said. "My mother said I could give her a farewell party."

"Neat. Who're you going to ask?"

"The class."

"The whole class!" Isabelle said, astonished.

"Yep. My mother says she doesn't think it would be nice to leave anyone out."

"You mean Chauncey and Mary Eliza and everybody?" Isabelle said, remembering parties she'd been left out of.

"Yep. Everyone," said Jane.

"That's a lot of mouths to feed," Isabelle said. "Maybe my mother could help."

"That'd be nice."

Isabelle raced back and caught Mrs. Esposito just as she was putting on her jacket.

"How many people are there in the class?" Isabelle cried.

"Twenty-one, I think." Mrs. Esposito did a little

mental arithmetic. "Yes, that's right. Not counting me," she said, smiling.

Isabelle charged back into the hall.

"There are twenty-one people in the class," she told Jane. "Not counting Mrs. Esposito. Don't forget her. You don't want to leave her out, do you?"

"Oh, no," said Jane. "Thanks for reminding me."

Isabelle felt she had done her good deed for the day. Sort of like the Lone Ranger.

"You're welcome, Kemosabe," she said.

Chapter Ten

"Have you heard the news?" Mary Eliza popped out from behind her locker. "Sally Smith is moving!"

"I know. Jane told me," said Isabelle. "She's having a farewell party for Sally. She's inviting everyone."

"Everyone?" Mary Eliza drew herself up haughtily. "That's a lot."

"It's twenty-two, including Mrs. Esposito. My mother's helping Jane's mother." Isabelle aimed a neat blow in Mary Eliza's direction. "Only one cupcake to a person," she hissed. "That's the rule."

Mary Eliza backed off and hissed back, "I'm getting Sally's job!"

"What job?" Isabelle asked, knowing perfectly well what job.

"Art editor of *The Bee*." *The Bee* was the class paper. Some kids wanted to call it *The Bumble Bee* but that was voted down as being too buzzy.

"It just so happens I have a picture with me I drew only this morning." Mary Eliza dove down into her briefcase and pulled out a drawing of a girl in a ballet suit.

Mary Eliza was the only person in the fifth grade, maybe even in the entire school, who had a briefcase.

Isabelle squinted at the picture. "It looks just like you," she said, "only not as ugly." Then she put out her arms and soared in circles around Mary Eliza, making airplane noises, preparing for takeoff.

Insults bounced off Mary Eliza like bullets off Superman. "It's interesting you should say that, because it *is* me," Mary Eliza said with pride. "A good likeness, if I do say so. Notice the placement of the feet, how the arm is extended. Perfect form. I am the artist as well as the artist's model. You might say I'm a shoo-in to be the new art editor of *The Bee*."

"*You* might but you won't catch me saying it," Isabelle said. "I wouldn't say you were a shoo-in if you tied me to a tree and poured honey on my nose so the ants would lick me to death."

"Ants can't lick you to death," Mary Eliza said,

crossing her arms on her chest and slitting her eyes, getting ready to pounce.

Isabelle backed off. She wondered if it was possible to run backwards. She'd never find out until she gave it a try. Moving backwards, she picked up speed.

"Hey! Watch where you're going!" Herbie hollered, as she bumped into him.

"Oh, hi. I thought you were still sick," Isabelle said. "I thought maybe your mother locked you in so the germs couldn't find you."

"She wanted to, but I told her if I missed any more school, I might get left back. So she wrote a note to excuse me from recess and gym so I wouldn't get overheated," Herbie explained.

"I thought only cars got overheated," Isabelle said. "I didn't know people did too."

"There's your little brother!" Mary Eliza shouted as Guy came down the hall.

"She doesn't have any little brother," Herbie said, scowling.

"I knew it! I knew it!" Mary Eliza cried.

"You can come to my house today if you want," Guy said. "My mother said it's all right."

"Today's my last day to do the route," Isabelle said. "Philip owes me a buck fifty times two."

"A buck fifty times two!" Herbie whistled.

"Whose little brother is he, then?"

"Go paint yourself into a corner, why don't you?" Isabelle suggested.

Mary Eliza twirled a few times to clear her head. "I might just do that," she said. "A portrait of the artist sitting in a corner. Another first for me."

"How about sitting on a tuffet, eating your curds and whey?" Herbie said.

"What's a tuffet?" Mary Eliza said.

"You don't know what a tuffet is?" Isabelle exclaimed, popping her eyes out.

"I bet you don't know what a tuffet is either, smarty pants. What's a tuffet, then?" Mary Eliza yelled.

"I'm not telling," Isabelle said. She made herself stand quietly and smile at Mary Eliza. It was easier to smile than it was to stand quietly. Much easier. But she did it. Then she turned and walked away—walked, not ran. All the way down the hall, she felt Mary Eliza's eyes on her.

Slowly, slowly. Walk, do not run.

Once around the corner she broke into a fifty-yard dash.

"Slow down!" she heard someone yell.

A sixth-grade traffic cop, the worst kind. Isabelle slowed down, feeling, in some way, victorious.

What *is* a tuffet anyway?

Chapter Eleven

"Mother, this is Herbie and this is Isabelle," Guy said.

"I've met Isabelle," Guy's mother said, not exactly unfriendly, but not exactly friendly, either. "Hello, Herbie," she said.

Herbie was not at his best in front of strangers. He mumbled hello back and hid behind Isabelle.

"Would you like some juice and crackers, children? Guy, you may pour the apple juice and Becca will get the crackers."

"Read any good books lately?" Isabelle asked Becca, joking.

Becca sighed elaborately and handed Isabelle a graham cracker.

Isabelle felt Herbie tugging on her. She reached around and slapped at him to cut it out.

Herbie drank two glasses of apple juice as if he'd just come from the desert. "Okay, where's the hot water?" he demanded, wiping his mouth on the back of his hand.

"If you'd like to wash your hands, Guy will show you to the lavatory," Guy's mother said.

"Outside, I meant." Herbie slid halfway under the table as all eyes turned on him.

"There's no hot water outside, only inside," Becca said.

"I know what he means," Guy said, coming to Herbie's rescue. "When my father first said we were moving here, I dreamed that I fished out of my bedroom window. Just let the line down and lots of fish swimming under my window bit and I hauled 'em up and ate them right there on the rug. They were delicious," he said dreamily. "I thought that was the way it was going to be, a little stream filled with hot water running under my window. I was disappointed for quite a long time."

"That's what I meant," Herbie said. "I thought hot water ran down the street." He didn't say he was disappointed too, but Isabelle thought he was.

"You want to see my chains?" Becca asked Herbie, having taken a sudden fancy to him.

Herbie blinked. "What kind of chains?"

"Chain chains," Becca said. "Come on."

Herbie went reluctantly, sticking his thumbs in his belt and walking like a cowboy, which wasn't easy considering he was wearing his old sneakers. Wait'll he found out what all those dangling chains meant! Herbie'd freak out, Isabelle was sure. He'd only read about one book in his whole life. Every time he had to give an oral book report, he got up and said, "This is a story of a boy who was raised in the wild."

Last time he'd pulled that, the class had groaned in unison.

"That will be quite enough, boys and girls," Mrs. Esposito had said, trying not to smile.

Guy went upstairs to change his clothes before going out to play. That left Isabelle alone with Guy's mother. Isabelle considered doing a tap dance to entertain Guy's mother and started moving her feet, getting them warmed up.

"You're not in Guy's class, are you?" his mother said.

"Nope. I'm in fifth grade," Isabelle replied.

"I thought you were too tall to be in the third grade. And Herbie? Is he in fifth grade too?"

Isabelle nodded.

"I would like Guy to have some friends his own age," Guy's mother said.

"Oh, he will," Isabelle said grandly. "Just wait. Once he gets toughened up, he'll have plenty of friends his own age."

Guy's mother raised her eyebrows. "Toughened up?" she said.

"Can I go up and see if he's ready yet?" Isabelle asked, wishing Herbie would come out of Becca's chain room and that Guy would come down in his old clothes and they could get the show on the road.

Guy came clattering downstairs just then, and Isabelle breathed a sigh of relief. Herbie came back too, looking stunned by his experience.

"He's only read thirty-five books," Becca told her mother. Isabelle glared at Herbie but he refused to meet her eyes. They both said "Thanks" to Guy's mother and traipsed outside.

"Thirty-five!" Isabelle leaned on Herbie so hard he almost fell. "Who are you kidding?"

"How many books have you read?" Herbie asked Guy.

Guy looked at the sky, counting. "Oh, about a hundred, I guess," he said.

"Have you got paper chains, too, in your room?"

"Some. Not as many as Becca. She's a show-off."

"How come you read so many books? How come your sister can read and she's only six?" Isabelle asked.

"Well, she's a gifted child," Guy said.

Herbie's eyes popped. "You shoulda told me!" he

wheezed. "I never woulda gone into her room to see the chains if I knew that."

"And also," Guy said, "my mother read to us while we were still inside her stomach. That way, she figured we'd get started early."

Astounded at this piece of information, Isabelle said, "Could you hear her?"

"I don't remember," Guy said truthfully. "I must've, though. My mother's a librarian, too."

"Oh." Isabelle nodded wisely. "That explains it." Herbie nodded wisely, too. They both felt better, knowing Guy and Becca's mother was a librarian.

"Bet she's always telling you to be quiet, huh?" Isabelle said, laughing.

Guy put his hand over his mouth and laughed through it, the way he did when he didn't get something.

"Don't you like to read?" he asked.

"I'd rather fight," said Isabelle.

"Can't you do both?"

Isabelle looked at the ground, then up at both boys. The thought had never occurred to her.

"I guess," she said, doubtfully.

Chapter Twelve

"I corrected them all, like you said. Check it." Isabelle thrust her arithmetic test under Mrs. Esposito's nose. "Please."

With her coat still on, Mrs. Esposito checked.

"Perfect," she said. "Now I want to see you do this the first time around next time. You can do as well. Can't you?"

"I'm not sure. I guess." Isabelle thought a minute "Sure."

"That's the way. Now would you mind opening the

window a trifle? This room smells like bologna sand-wiches."

"Don't you like bologna sandwiches?"

"Not enough to smell them all morning."

Isabelle flung open the window, sending the papers on Mrs. Esposito's desk flying.

"I said a trifle, not the whole way."

Isabelle closed the window to a slit and picked up the papers.

"If they called you a goody-goody because you never did anything wrong, never even had to go to the prin-cipal's office once," she said suddenly, "and kids teased you and chased you and called you names, what would you do?" Isabelle watched Mrs. Esposito with her bright brown eyes and waited to hear what she'd say.

"That's a tough one," Mrs. Esposito said, frowning. "I assume you're not talking about yourself, Isabelle," she said, winking.

"It's a friend of mine." Isabelle didn't feel like jok-ing. "It's this really nice little guy. He's, well, he's sort of, well, sweet. I really like him. I feel bad because these crummy creeps make him miserable and there's nothing he can do about it. I tried to teach him how to fight so he can punch 'em out, but he doesn't like to fight. How can he be mean and tough if he's not mean or tough?"

"He probably can't. How old is he?"

"He's only eight."

"Give him a while. Maybe he'll figure out some-thing in a couple of years."

"Yeah, but what does he do for a couple of years? Just stand there and take it?"

"Perhaps the best thing would be to tell his mother and father, and they could handle it," Mrs. Esposito suggested.

"He doesn't want to do that. You know how moth-ers and fathers are." Isabelle lifted her shoulders and turned her hands palms up, trying to explain mothers and fathers to her teacher.

"They're supposed to protect children until chil-dren are big enough to take care of themselves," Mrs. Esposito said. "I think eight is too little to handle something like this by himself. Why don't you tell your friend to tell his parents and they might be able to help."

Isabelle shook her head from side to side, letting her brown hair swing across her cheeks. "He won't," she said firmly. "I know this kid and I guarantee you, he won't."

A little knock came at the door. "Come in," the teacher called. The door opened and Guy stood there, hair slicked down, cowlick waving from the top of his head. His cheeks were shiny with soap.

"I came to talk to her," Guy said, pointing to Isa-belle.

"Well, talk then," Isabelle said. He looked very

small to her. Very clean and very small.

"Did you figure out anything yet?" He came right up to her and whispered, so Mrs. Esposito wouldn't hear. "You promised. Did you?"

"Not yet," Isabelle said.

"I thought so." Guy stuck his hands in his pockets and dug the toe of his sneaker against the nearest desk. "I was counting on you." He looked at her with his enormous eyes. "If you can't figure out something, then I guess nobody can."

Isabelle's face got warm. She was blushing. She tried to think of something to say to make Guy feel better and couldn't.

"Guess what!" Chauncey Lapidus charged into the room like a bull. Or a steamroller. "I'm invited to a party!" He looked around at their faces, wanting them to share his joy and pleasure at this singular event. "I'm invited to Sally Smith's farewell party! I never been invited to a party before. But I'm going to this one!" Chauncey's face glowed.

"Oh, everybody's going to the party for Sally Smith," Isabelle said airily. "The whole class is invited."

Chauncey's face fell.

"How nice, Chauncey!" Mrs. Esposito cried. "I like parties, too."

When Chauncey stomped to his desk at the back of the room, Mrs. Esposito said in a low voice, "That wasn't nice, Isabelle. That was unkind and you know it. Why couldn't you let him enjoy his invitation without telling him everyone was going? I'm ashamed of you."

Isabelle's head drooped like a wilted flower on a stalk. Tears stung her eyes. She knew she shouldn't have said what she said. Chauncey felt special, being invited to the party. And she'd destroyed that feeling. Isabelle raised her head, peeking up at Mrs. Esposito's feet tucked neatly under her desk. Mrs. Esposito didn't raise her eyes. Isabelle checked out the hall. It was empty. Guy had gone. The day had just begun.

When the recess bell rang, the entire class rose as one and exited, shouting and screaming their joy at being released. Isabelle stayed behind.

"I didn't mean to be mean," she said to Mrs. Esposito.

Mrs. Esposito regarded her steadily. "Are you sure?"

"I'm sure I'm sure," Isabelle said, enjoying the rhythm of her words. "I'm very sure I'm sure."

"This is not a joke, Isabelle. This is serious. Think about it for a while. On the one hand, you're trying to help your friend Guy out of his problem. And on the other, you're making another boy unhappy. To be mean for meanness' sake is a terrible thing. You wanted to put Chauncey down. You knew exactly what to say to bring this about. I'm disappointed in you. Now, I'm afraid I have work to do." Mrs. Esposito bent over her desk, shutting Isabelle out.

What do I care? Isabelle thought. She ran, shouting and screaming as loud as anybody, out to the playground, looking for some action.

Chapter Thirteen

"How do you like it?" Mrs. Stern asked, pointing to her tomato-red front door. "I think it's the best I've ever done. Mixed it myself, too. Mr. Brady across the street told me when he comes out on his way to work and sees that door, it makes his day. Come on in, both of you."

Isabelle and Guy followed her down the hall to the kitchen. "This is my friend Guy Gibbs," Isabelle said. "He's a customer on my route. This is my last day to deliver. Philip's off his crutches, darn it. I was hoping he'd have to use 'em a lot longer."

"Hello, Guy. One or two?" Mrs. Stern bustled about, getting down a bag of marshmallows.

"What are they?" Guy whispered.

"Marshmallows, dummy." Isabelle said. "Take two, I'll eat yours."

"Two, please," Guy said.

"Well, this is indeed a pleasure." Mrs. Stern's silver eyes twinkled. "I haven't seen you in so long I thought you'd forgotten me."

"I've been here but you were always someplace else," Isabelle said.

"To tell you the truth, an old friend is in town," Mrs. Stern said. "He's been taking me dancing and to the movies and the museums. Oh, it's been grand!" She clasped her hands, a dreamy expression on her face. "It's been lovely," she said.

Isabelle was astonished. She had thought Mrs. Stern was an old lady. A very sharp old lady, but nevertheless an old lady. And now she was behaving like a teenager. Well, the dancing and the movies were teenage things. She wasn't sure about the museums.

Mrs. Stern poured out the cocoa and sat down with them. Marshmallows bobbed cozily on the hot cocoa. "Is he your age?" Isabelle asked, having decided it was better not to say, "Is he as old as you?"

"No, he's older." Mrs. Stern punched down her marshmallow with her spoon. Isabelle let out a little gasp. Mrs. Stern grinned.

"I knew that'd get you!" Mrs. Stern laughed. "He's the older brother of my dearest friend. When she died, she left me a ring in her will, and he came to deliver it personally."

"Did that make you sad?" Isabelle asked.

"We had been friends for almost sixty years," Mrs. Stern said simply.

Isabelle and Guy looked at one another and said nothing.

"Tell me about you," Mrs. Stern said briskly, looking straight at Guy. To put off answering her, he put both marshmallows into his mouth at once. It was more than he could handle. Mrs. Stern tactfully left the table.

"Spit 'em out!" Isabelle ordered. Guy's aim was good. The slightly soggy marshmallows landed neatly in his cup.

"More cocoa?" Mrs. Stern said.

Guy nodded, incapable of speech at the moment.

"He lives on Hot Water Street," Isabelle said. "He's in third grade. His sister is six. She reads books. His father is a football coach. His mother is a librarian."

"Well," Mrs. Stern said, after a small silence, "I guess that takes care of Guy. How is life treating you, Isabelle?"

"So so," Isabelle said, shrugging. "Pretty good. Not great."

Guy sat up very straight. "Maybe you and my grandmother could be friends," he said suddenly.

"She's about your age. She comes and stays with us sometimes. Her name is Maybelle Gibbs."

"I hope someday we may meet," Mrs. Stern said. "That's very kind of you to think of, Guy."

Isabelle rolled her eyes at Guy. "We better go now," she said. "I have lots of papers to deliver."

"Don't be such a stranger, Isabelle, even if Philip is back on his feet," Mrs. Stern said. "I've missed you. You come again too, Guy."

"What'd you say that for?" Isabelle demanded when they were outside. "What a dumb thing to say. Telling Mrs. Stern she was about the same age as your grandmother. Sheesh!"

"What's so dumb about that?" Unexpectedly, Guy defended himself. "She said her best friend died, didn't she? So I thought my grandmother and her could be best friends. What's so dumb about that?"

"Oh, come on. Quit dragging your feet." Isabelle stalked ahead angrily. Mrs. Stern had said that Guy was kind. She'd never said Isabelle was kind. Isabelle wished she'd thought of suggesting Guy's grandmother and Mrs. Stern might be friends. Then Mrs. Stern might've smiled at her and told her she was kind.

"Tell your mother I'm collecting today," Isabelle directed when they reached Guy's house.

"She's not home. My grandmother's staying with us. My mother's working," he said.

Isabelle heard Becca playing the piano. She tiptoed

to a window and peeked in. I wonder how they got it inside, she thought. If I ever run into those moving men, I'll ask. I wonder if they took off the legs.

When she turned, Guy was right behind her.

"Did you think of anything yet?" he asked.

"Nope," she said. "Maybe you better ask your mother and father if they can figure out how to make those geezers stop teasing you."

Guy's face crumpled. "My mother and father?" he said in a cracked voice. "I counted on you." All of him drooped, including his cowlick. "I counted on you, Isabelle," he said.

Isabelle hoisted her newspaper bag from one shoulder to the other. Guy held one hand over his mouth. Over it, his huge eyes looked at her, unblinking.

"Well," she said in a gruff voice, "maybe I'll come up with something. But don't stand on one leg until I do, okay?"

The corners of Guy's mouth turned up a little. He put one hand on Isabelle's arm where it rested, as weightless as a leaf.

"You're my friend," he said. "My best friend, Isabelle."

"Pooh!" Isabelle cried. She turned and ran, as fast as she could, as if she were running in the fifty-yard dash, the canvas bag thumping rhythmically against her back. Guy waved at her but she never once looked back.

"Jane Malone's mother is having a farewell party for Sally Smith. The whole class is invited. I said you'd help," Isabelle gasped, bursting into the kitchen.

"You remember Mrs. Stilson, Isabelle," Isabelle's mother said in her "mind your manners" tone.

"Sure. Hello, Mrs. Stilson."

"Hello, Isabelle." Mrs. Stilson's stomach billowed under her maternity dress.

"I didn't know you were having a baby," Isabelle said. "When's it coming?" She almost pointed at Mrs. Stilson's stomach but stopped herself in time. Beside her, she heard her mother sigh.

"In five weeks," Mrs. Stilson replied.

Isabelle pondered this information.

"You want me to read to it?" she said at last.

"That would be nice." Mrs. Stilson looked startled.

"Isabelle loves babies," her mother said. One never knew what Isabelle might say. One often wished Isabelle would keep her trap shut.

"I'll read to it right now," Isabelle announced.

"Okay," Mrs. Stilson said.

"I think I'll go down to the cellar and do a load of wash," Isabelle's mother said. She sometimes did this when Isabelle got to be too much for her. Isabelle dashed up to her room and dashed back, bearing her favorite Dr. Seuss.

"Did you know if you read to your baby while it's still in your stomach, it'll probably be an ace reader when it gets out?"

Mrs. Stilson digested this information while Isabelle sat and aimed herself at Mrs. Stilson's stomach. In a loud and penetrating voice, Isabelle pronounced each word very clearly so the baby would hear each one.

"There you are," Guy's grandmother said.

"Where'd you think I was?"

She raised her eyebrows. "Something wrong?" she asked.

"No," Guy said.

Becca came in and said, "Did you hear me practicing the piano?"

"Yeah," Guy said, "you stink."

"Guy, what's come over you?" his grandmother said.

Becca sat down at the table with her crayons and began coloring Snoopy's nose bright red.

"He's just mad because he doesn't have any friends," Becca said.

"That'll be enough, miss," Guy's grandmother said.

Calmly Becca colored Snoopy's ears purple.

"You may be a gifted child but you sure are a lousy colorer," Guy told her.

"I have three friends. Their names are Donna and Michelle and Amy." Becca colored Snoopy's arms and legs yellow.

"Yeah, well, I have three friends too," Guy said. "Their names are Isabelle and Herbie and Mrs. Stern."

"Friends are supposed to be the same age you are,"

Becca said. "Isabelle and Herbie are older'n you. I don't know any Mrs. Stern."

"Yeah, well, she's the same age I am," Guy said.

Becca opened her mouth, then closed it and went back to her piano.

"Well done," Guy's grandmother told him.

Chapter Fourteen

The day of the party dawned bright and clear. Isabelle bounded out of bed, wrote PARTY! for the fifth time on her blackboard, then bounded downstairs.

Isabelle's mother stood at the sink, stabbing at a floating eggshell. "What time's the movie let out?"

"I can walk home," Philip said.

"Where's he going?" Isabelle rested her elbows on the table.

"It's none of your business!" Philip shot one of his laser-beam stares at her, guaranteed to cut her in half.

"There's a bunch of people going. We'll walk home together."

"Does he have a date?" Isabelle asked her mother.

Philip's face went from pink to red to purple. Once, years ago, Philip had had a tantrum. He might be having another, Isabelle thought, shivering in anticipation.

"Shut your face," he ordered, from the corner of his mouth.

"I forgot," he said, remembering. "Billy's brother is picking us up when it's over."

"Is he the one who's been arrested for speeding?"

"No, that's Chuck's brother," Isabelle said. "He plays cool disco," and she did a brief disco dance to illustrate.

Philip unclenched his hands and went for Isabelle's throat.

"Good morning." Isabelle's father, all suited up for work, greeted his happy little family. "What's up?" he asked, snapping open his newspaper, reaching for his coffee.

"Philip has a date," Isabelle said. "With a girl."

Philip made a gargling noise. Isabelle picked up her bowl and drank the remaining milk. No one told her not to. This day was off to a fine start. Invigorated, she jogged outside, looking for Guy. He wasn't there. She jogged all the way to school, turning now and then to see if he was following her. He wasn't in the playground either. Just as well. She still hadn't come up with a solution. After the party she would. She promised herself she would.

"Class, we all know today is the big sendoff for Sally," Mrs. Esposito said. "Tomorrow, we're going to hold an election to see who will fill Sally's shoes." Chauncey stuck one leg straight up in the air and wiggled his foot. Everybody laughed, then looked at Sally. She only smiled and bent over her book. Sally Smith was a star. She not only was art editor, she was lots of other things. Everyone wanted to be Sally Smith.

Mary Eliza flipped back her hair and preened like a peacock. Isabelle studied her Adidas. Sally's feet were small and hers were big. Still, she knew she could fill Sally's shoes nicely. It would be grand to be an art editor. Even if she didn't know what one did.

"Each of you is allowed one vote," Mrs. Esposito went on. "Drop your votes in here," and she pointed to the box on her desk. It was the box that served as a Valentine box on Valentine's Day, and it had a large, faded red heart pasted on its front.

"I want you to vote for the person you think will do the best job," Mrs. Esposito told them. "Don't vote for yourself unless you're prepared to work hard." A wave of snickers rolled over the room. Isabelle shot one of her laser beams in Mary Eliza's direction. But Mary Eliza was so busy looking modest, she didn't notice.

The party got off to a good start. Chauncey kicked a soccer ball which landed smack in Mary Eliza's mouth, jarring her retainer and sending blood spurting down her chin. Mary Eliza was brave and poor Chauncey felt terrible. When the excitement had died down, refreshments were served. Isabelle's mother's cupcakes were a big hit. Isabelle was extremely proud of her mother and told everyone whose cupcakes they were. The high spot was when Mrs. Malone brought out a large chocolate three-layer cake with FAREWELL, SALLY written on it in pink icing.

"Here, Sally," she said, handing Sally a cake knife, "you do the honors."

With a big smile, Sally cut the first slice. Then, to everyone's amazement, she burst into tears.

"Oh, dear," Mrs. Malone said. "What's wrong, dear? Do you feel all right?"

"I feel fine," Sally blubbered. "It's just that I hate to move. I'm sad about leaving. I don't want to go."

Isabelle was dismayed by Sally's tears. She didn't think Sally ever cried. Sally was a leader. Leaders didn't cry.

"Nothing will ever be as nice as here," Sally snuffled. "This is the best place in the world. Nothing will be as much fun."

"Don't worry, Sally," Isabelle said. "You'll make friends. I bet you'll be the art editor at your new school. I bet you'll be the best speller and the best in arithmetic, too."

"I don't want to be a baby," Sally said. "But I couldn't help it."

"I'll miss you," Isabelle whispered at the edge of Sally's ear. "You are my friend, Sally. You are the best person in the entire world. You are the best . . ." she paused, trying to think of other comforting words to offer Sally. Herbie arrived and stepped hard on Isabelle's Adidas.

"Knock it off," Herbie said, scowling. "We're having a game of musical chairs, so come on and stop being a jerk."

Musical chairs! Isabelle's favorite. All the pushing and shoving! Lovely.

"Come on, Sally," and Isabelle dragged her new friend's hand and pulled her into the game.

Isabelle had never even been to Sally's house. She had not been invited to Sally's birthday party, which took place in Sally's rec room. Sally had one toe out the door, so to speak, and here they were, best friends. She promised to write her every day.

That night, before lights out, Isabelle wrote on her blackboard SALLY SMITH IS COOL. SALLY SMITH IS MY PEN PAL. SALLY SMITH IS MY NEW BEST FRIEND.

And underneath, written in letters so small she had to push her nose against the blackboard to read them, Isabelle wrote: YEAH! ISABELLE, NEW ART ED. OF THE BEE. YEAH!

Chapter Fifteen

"They followed me home from school yesterday," Guy said. "Calling me goody-goody Guy, Mama's boy, all that. I went to your house and you weren't there. I sat and waited for you and you didn't come."

"I was at Sally Smith's farewell party," Isabelle told him. "I told you about that. You knew I was going to her party. I can't just not go because you want me to figure out a way to make 'em stop, can I?"

"No," said Guy.

"I thought about it, though. A lot. I thought and

thought. How about if you throw a stone through the principal's window. And it breaks. Not a big stone, only a little one, so if it hit Mrs. Prendergast, it would only bounce off her head and wouldn't even cut her or anything. Only scare her a little. How about that?" asked Isabelle, who had only just that minute thought of this plan.

"My father'd get awful mad at me if I did that," Guy said. "Besides, I like Mrs. Prendergast. She never did anything to me. Why'd I want to do that to her?"

"For crying out loud!" Isabelle cried. "What difference does it make if you like her or not? You want them to stop calling you names, don't you? You want to do something bad so they won't call you a goody-goody, don't you?"

"Yes," said Guy.

"Well then. If you did that, everybody would find out about it and they'd say, 'Hey, that's the little creep we were always calling a goody-goody. Guess he's not one after all.' Isn't that what you want?"

"I'm too scared to do something like that," Guy said.

"Well, you could break into the school on Saturday when it was empty and write stuff on the walls and mess up the classrooms." He looked at her with great, sad eyes and was silent.

"Sheesh! I'm running out of ideas," Isabelle said.

"That's okay. I know you tried. Maybe my grandmother will think of something."

"Your grandmother?" Isabelle stood on her head. "Your grandmother?" She liked the way the words came out when she talked standing on her head. They sounded odd, not like her at all. "I'll bet she doesn't know squat about getting into trouble."

"She was a child once," Guy said.

"Yeah, like about a hundred million years ago." Spots began to dance in front of Isabelle's eyes, but she stayed put.

"She may be old," Guy defended his grandmother, "but she's young at heart." He'd heard that in a song on the radio once and thought it described his grandmother perfectly.

Isabelle collapsed and lay outstretched on the ground. At that instant Herbie's mother drove by. Herbie leaned out and yelled, "Hey, you finally got her! Yippee!" and the car kept going until it was out of sight.

Made bold by this, Guy planted one of his feet firmly on Isabelle's stomach, holding her down. "How about you and me fighting?" he asked, tempted to put both feet on her and take a little walk. But he wasn't *that* bold.

"You whippersnapper!" Isabelle hollered, struggling to get up. Guy removed his foot and started running. He wanted to put distance between himself and her.

When he looked back, she was standing there, shaking her fist at him. "You bozo!" she cried.

Elated by an unaccustomed feeling of power, Guy waved and kept on going. He'd never stepped on anyone in his entire life. It was an exhilarating experience.

When Guy got home, his grandmother was soaking her feet in Epsom salts.

"My dogs are barking," she said, rubbing one dripping foot against the other.

Becca turned her head, listening. "I don't hear anything," she said.

"She means her feet hurt, you whippersnapper," said Guy.

"You're getting feisty," his grandmother said. "I detect the influence of the paper boy."

"When you were a child, were you ever bad?" Guy asked suddenly.

"Once in a while. The worst thing I ever did was try to sell my baby sister to some new people who moved on our street." She threw back her head and laughed. "I wasn't very old, only about four. And I was very jealous of my sister. She was getting entirely too much attention, it seemed to me. So when the new people moved in, I bundled up the baby and pushed her in her pram down the street. I rang the bell, and when the lady of the house came to the door, I said, 'Would you like to buy this baby? She's for sale. Cheap.' I'll tell you, they never let me forget that."

"Did they buy the baby?" Guy wanted to know. He was entranced with the story. If only he'd thought of that when Becca was little. It was too late now, of course. Nobody would want to buy a gifted child.

"No. They had children of their own. I would've tried it again but they kept a close eye on me from then on. Then there was the time I took my brother's bicycle. Molly McCabe and I wanted to go on a picnic. I guess I had a bicycle, but the tires were flat or some such thing. Anyway, I took Bob's. He was older than I and had a terrible temper. As luck would have it, he came home and wanted to ride his bicycle. And it was gone. Well, there was some fracas when Bob discovered I'd taken it, I can tell you. I was shut in my room without supper that night. We'd always been taught to respect other people's property, you see. That was a fair old time. What fun we had! We never did anything really bad. Not like some of the things that happen these days."

Guy sat still, hoping she'd think of some other tales of her childhood. None of them were of any use to him, of course, except for the baby-selling one. If only he'd thought of that before Becca could talk. Come to think of it, she'd been born talking. Life was full of missed opportunities, it seemed to him.

"This water's getting chilly," Guy's grandmother said. "I better dry my feet before I take cold. Bring me a towel, would you please, Guy?"

He sat on the floor and watched while she dried her

feet. Her legs were very white. Blue veins ran every which way up and down them, then trailed a slender tracing across her feet.

"Did you ever get sent to the principal's office?" Guy wanted to know.

"Once or twice. Our principal was an old lady who wore glasses and her skirts to the floor. She looked like somebody's grandmother. But she was tough." Guy's grandmother rolled her eyes at him. "My Lord, but she was tough. Nobody got away with anything with her. She was allowed to cane the boys and not the girls. Those were the days, you see, when girls were supposed to be the gentler sex. We both know that's not the case, don't we?" Guy nodded, afraid to speak, afraid to break the spell.

"She'd say to me, 'Maybelle, it pains me to see you here again,' meaning her office. She knew my name, you see, knew the name of every child in the school. And their family situation, too. She was a very smart woman. Hand me my slippers, will you, Guy?"

He handed them to her and said, without thinking, "I like you."

"I like you too," she said.

"I'm not much for kissing," he told her, so there'd be no misunderstanding.

"How about hugging?"

He thought about that. "I guess hugging's okay as long as you don't hug too hard or too much."

"Listen," she said, "I've had lots of experience. I

always hug just right." He allowed her to give him a sample.

"How was it?" she asked.

"Just right," Guy said.

Chapter Sixteen

The afternoon stretched slowly, slowly, like Rip van Winkle waking from his twenty years' sleep. The clock seemed to have stopped ticking. A fat black fly beat its head against the window. Outside, someone tried repeatedly and unsuccessfully to start a car's engine. Inside, Isabelle read about how many coffee beans there were in Brazil.

Something was crawling around inside her T-shirt. Isabelle pulled it away from herself with one finger and peered down. There was nothing there except her undershirt. She hooked the T-shirt over her nose and looked out at the room over it, hoping someone was watching her.

Mary Eliza Shook was paying close attention to her book. Isabelle made a few faces in that direction, but Mary Eliza never once looked up. So Isabelle crossed her eyes at Herbie over her T-shirt. But Herbie was involved in making a spitball and didn't even notice.

Mrs. Esposito cleared her throat loudly. Everyone jumped. Mrs. Esposito glared at Isabelle, who took her T-shirt down from her nose and went back to Brazil.

"All right, class. You can put away your books now." At last Mrs. Esposito took pity on them. A great crashing and banging followed her announcement. They were ready.

"I have counted all the votes and I'm happy to announce the name of the new art editor," Mrs. Esposito said.

Everyone sat up very straight, trying not to look self-conscious. A couple of kids in back starting horsing around.

"There will be no announcement, class, until everyone comes to order," Mrs. Esposito said.

I bet she'd make a good army person, Isabelle thought in admiration. They wouldn't dare disobey Mrs. Esposito.

When at last the class was totally still, Mrs. Esposito said, "When I announce the winner's name, I would like that person to stand, please."

Isabelle got her feet ready.

"Our new art editor is . . ."

Isabelle closed her eyes and clasped her hands in front of her, as if she were praying.

Mary Eliza lifted her backside off her chair, ready to spring.

Mrs. Esposito's voice seemed to come from the end of a long tunnel.

"Our new art editor is . . ." Mrs. Esposito liked to tantalize them.

"Herbie!" she cried.

Isabelle's eyes snapped open, and she said, "Herbie?"

Herbie looked as if he'd been hit over the head with a shovel.

"Herbie!" yelled Herbie. "That's cuckoo! I don't want to be no art editor! I won't—"

"Will the winner please stand?" Mrs. Esposito said, in measured tones. The boy sitting behind Herbie punched him in the back and growled, "Stand up, wonko."

Hitching up his pants, Herbie staggered to his feet, his orange-juice mustache giving him a somewhat sinister look.

"Congratulations, Herbie," said Mrs. Esposito. "We know you'll do a good job. And class, it's my pleasure to tell you that Herbie had more votes than any other candidate. Let's give him three cheers."

"Hip hip hooray!" the class thundered, three times. Herbie sat down and his expression was one of total amazement.

"I don't know what happened," he mumbled. He shook his head once or twice, like a boxer down for the count. "I don't want to be no art editor. I don't know what an art editor's supposed to do, so how can I do it?"

"I'll give you a hand, Herb," Isabelle soothed him. "I'll be your right-hand man."

"Yeah, but how about my left hand? My left hand needs help, too." Herbie was definitely in the pits.

"If you ask me," Mary Eliza stormed up, "it's a put-up job."

"So who asked you?" Imitating prizefighters she'd seen on TV, Isabelle dabbed at her nose with her thumb several times.

In a rage, Mary Eliza flounced away without speaking.

"All I know is," Herbie said glumly, "it musta been somebody who hates me. Who else would vote for me? They knew I didn't want the job. I have an enemy and I didn't even know it." Herbie's face wore a hunted look.

"It wasn't me, Herb," Isabelle said. "You can count on that."

"You're a pal, Iz." Herbie called Isabelle Iz when his emotions were stirred. "Thanks for not voting for me. You voted for yourself, right?"

"Sure. Who else would've?" She took a few pokes at him, trying to cheer him up. Herbie was not in a laughing mood, however.

"Wait'll my mother hears I'm art editor," Herbie said. "She'll flip."

"How about if we have a good fight? That'll make you feel better," Isabelle suggested.

"No, thanks. I'm not in the mood," Herbie said. "I'm going home."

"What're you gonna do when you get home?" Isabelle wanted to know.

He looked at her, his eyes full of woe. "Think," he said.

"Think?" Isabelle echoed.

"Yeah, think."

"Awesome," said Isabelle.

Chapter Seventeen

"Take that! And that! And that!" Guy shadow-boxed his way around his room, ferocious, fearless, unbeatable. Bouncing on the balls of his feet, fists held up the way Isabelle had taught him, Guy smiled quietly at his own power.

Last night he'd watched a karate exhibition on TV. Those guys knew what was what. He'd seen a girl smaller than he was break a board with her bare hands. Imagine that. If she could, he could.

"I'm gonna knock you out of your socks," Guy muttered. "I'm gonna bash in your head and stick my thumb in your eye, and when it falls out I'm just gonna leave it there. I'm not gonna pick it up or anything, just leave it there." He shivered, thinking of all those eyes lying on the ground, looking up at him.

It was all very well to be mean and tough in your own room, in your own house with all your family there. It was another thing entirely, Guy knew, to be mean and tough out in the real world, when and where it counted.

Karate was the answer, no question. All he had to do was talk his mother and father into letting him take a karate course. They had one at the Y.

Someone knocked. Guy said, "Come in," in a deep and hairy voice. It was Herbie.

"Your mom said I could come up," Herbie said.

"I was just practicing," Guy said.

Herbie sat on the bed. "I got elected art editor of *The Bee* today," he said.

"That's nice," Guy said. "You wanna do anything? Look through my microscope or anything? Look at my stamp collection?"

Herbie shook his head no.

"My favorite animal is frogs," Guy said. "What's yours?"

"Zebra," Herbie answered, after some thought.

"I never saw a zebra," Guy said.

"Me either," said Herbie. "Except on a jungle special."

"Want some Jell-O?" he asked Guy, pulling a packet out of his pocket.

"What color?"

"Green." Herbie ripped open the inside wrapping and poured out some green Jell-O into his hand. "Once I used it to brush my teeth with," he said.

"What'd it taste like?"

"Green," Herbie said. He poured some into his mouth and some more into Guy's open hand. Guy wondered if he really wanted some Jell-O that bad.

"My second favorite animal is unicorns," he said.

"I never saw one, never heard of one either," Herbie said, chewing and making a face.

"It's got one horn growing out of its head. If you see one, it means good luck."

"One horn," Herbie said. "Crazy."

"I never even saw one in the zoo. That's because it's only mythical," Guy explained.

"What's that mean?"

"It isn't real. It doesn't really exist. It's just in your imagination."

"Crazy," Herbie said again.

There was a companionable silence as the two boys stared into space.

"I'm going to paint my room dark blue and paste stars on the ceiling," Guy said at last.

"Cool," said Herbie. "My mother put wallpaper on mine. It's stupid. It's stripes that go up and down, up and down. That's it. I wouldn't mind pasting stars on mine. Where you getting the stars?"

Guy shrugged. He hadn't thought it through. "Maybe from school," he said. "Like the ones they give you if you get an A. Silver stars. That way, I can look at 'em at night and pretend I'm sleeping out."

"Yeah. You can also get a jar full of mosquitoes, and when it gets dark, let 'em out. They'll dive-bomb you all night and bite the stuffing out of you. That way, you'll *really* think you're sleeping out." Herbie laughed and scratched himself on the leg.

Guy covered his mouth with his hand and smiled around it at Herbie. He liked the idea of sleeping out under the stars, but he wasn't too hot on the idea of mosquitoes.

Becca knocked and opened the door.

"Supper's ready," she announced.

"You wanna stay for supper?" Guy asked.

"What's for supper?"

"Tuna fish," said Becca.

Herbie only liked to stay at people's houses for supper if they were having spaghetti.

"No thanks," he said. "My mother said I should be home early. See you," he said.

Guy listened to the sound of Herbie's feet clattering down the stairs. Then he started punching his way around the room again.

"Take that and that and that!" he muttered.

Pow, pow, pow!

Not one mosquito escaped his deadly blows.

"Supper's ready!"

Stepping carefully around the mosquito bodies littering the floor, Guy went downstairs.

The first thing I have to do, he thought, is get some stars. Then I get the paint.

Chapter Eighteen

"It was me voted Herbie in," Chauncey bragged. *"I started* the landslide. Just the way when somebody runs for president. Some presidents win by only a couple of votes, and some win by a landslide. I told it around that Herbie was our man. I told 'em Herbie was the best person for the job. I landslided Herbie into office, I did." Chauncey beamed. Isabelle felt like wiping off Chauncey's smile. She got her fists ready.

"It was a good deed, huh?" she asked. "You Lone Ranger, me Tonto. Who Kemosabe?"

"Talk English, why don'tcha?" Power had already gone to Chauncey's head. He wasn't letting any grass grow under *his* feet, Isabelle thought.

She opened her mouth, ready to let him have it. Unbidden, Mrs. Esposito's words about being kind popped into her head. She shook it, trying to clear the words out. But they stayed, they wouldn't go away.

Chauncey was not an easy person to be kind to. But she had promised herself she'd try. So try she would.

She cleared her throat and said, "You did a good job, Chauncey."

Stunned by praise, to which he was a stranger, Chauncey puffed out his chest like a baby robin who's just caught the first worm of the season.

"I'm thinking of going into politics," he said. "I was going to be a tennis player or maybe a pro ball player, but now I've decided to go into politics. I'm even writing a speech."

Talk about getting the ball and running with it! Isabelle thought. "What about?" she said.

"Whaddya mean, what about?" Chauncey had lost his train of thought.

"The speech. What's it about?"

"Oh." Chauncey shrugged. "Lots of things."

"Name some."

Chauncey stared at a spot just over Isabelle's head. "Well, peace on earth, for one."

"Are you for it or against it?" Isabelle asked, dangling her hands loosely, the way Philip did before a swim meet.

"I'm for it," Chauncey said stoutly. "Plus, we oughta have more open spaces and less pollution. I think weekends oughta be longer. I think kids oughta have the same rights parents have. I think . . ."

"You're all right, Chauncey," Isabelle cut in. Once started, Chauncey had fallen in love with the sound of his own words.

"We should also have bigger lunches and not so much homework," he continued, glassy-eyed with joy at her attention. "I also think kids oughta be allowed to pick out their own shoes when they go to the shoe store. They have to wear 'em, not their mothers."

Chauncey was getting out of hand, Isabelle decided. "I'm late," she said. "See you."

"Hi," said Guy, as she rounded the steps to the playground. "Did you?"

"No," she said. "Not yet."

"Well, you don't have to. You said you were going to think of something. I didn't ask you, you said you would."

"I know. I will. I'm real busy right now." The sight of Guy looking woebegone made her feel guilty. "Listen, wait here. I've got something for you." She wanted to make him look happy so she wouldn't feel so bad. "I'll be right back."

And she was. "Here, these are for you."

Guy's eyes shone as he saw the five silver stars

she handed him. "Gee, thanks," he said.

"Mrs. Esposito said it was all she had left. She said she ordered some more. Maybe you can ask her later and she'll fork over some more. So long," and she left him in the hall, smiling at his stars.

After school Guy kept an eye out for Isabelle. Maybe they'd go see Mrs. Stern again. She was, Guy knew, a good mixer of paints. He knew just the shade of blue he wanted—a deep blue, the color the sky got just before total darkness fell, before the moon showed its face.

A boy named Bernie barreled out the door.

"Hey, Bernie," Guy said shyly. Bernie sat across the aisle from him. Bernie was small, smaller even than Guy. Bernie was very smart, too, but he didn't make a big deal out of being smart.

"My cat had kittens this morning," Bernie said, out of breath. "I was eating a piece of toast when the first one was born, right in our kitchen in my mother's old laundry basket."

"How many did she have?" Guy asked, envious, wishing he'd been there in Bernie's kitchen, eating toast when the first kitten was born.

Bernie held up three fingers. "My mother said to hurry home, maybe there'd be more. Gotta go!" and Bernie went.

Guy watched him go, wishing he was going too, running home to see Bernie's new kittens.

I don't need Isabelle, Guy thought. I can find Mrs.

Stern's by myself. I've been there once. Just keep an eye out for the tomato-red door.

Follow the yellow brick road. He'd seen *The Wizard of Oz* four times on television and wondered if he'd ever have the luck to find a yellow brick road. He thought not.

A solitary walk on a sunny day was not a bad thing. He'd find some violets, pick a bouquet for Mrs. Stern. This was violet time. He'd seen their little faces peeking out in empty lots he'd passed on his way to school. He was in no hurry. He liked being alone. Sometimes, not always. This was one of those times when he liked it a lot.

Guy started to skip. He was quite a good skipper, if he did say so himself.

This is the turn. Is this the turn? Surely this was Mrs. Stern's street. He wished he'd paid more attention when Isabelle and he had come here.

Still, he could find it on his own. He knew he could. But suppose Mrs. Stern had painted her front door another color? Isabelle had said she changed the colors of her rooms and her front door at the drop of a hat.

What then?

No, that door was still tomato-red. Hadn't Mrs. Stern said she liked that color, it was the best she'd ever done?

Guy investigated a spot of color he thought might be a clump of violets. No, it turned out to be only a piece of paper, crumpled up and thrown away.

Up ahead, a group of people were making a lot of noise, shouting and hollering. Guy heard loud voices, loud music. One of them had a big radio turned up high. They were too far away to give him any trouble, but Guy kept an eye on them anyway, just to make sure.

With a surge of relief Guy saw the red door. It shone at him like a beacon lighting his way. And even though he'd found no violets for Mrs. Stern, he hurried toward that red door, empty-handed and joyful. Would she ask him in for some cocoa? Maybe not. Maybe she only asked Isabelle in. No, she'd ask him in. He was positive.

He knocked, getting a big smile ready to greet her. Maybe she wouldn't remember him. He knocked twice, getting anxious. Sure she would. She was a nice lady. She'd remember him. If she didn't, he'd tell her he was Isabelle's friend. Then she'd ask him in. For sure.

Should he knock again? Someone was watching him. He felt eyes. Maybe Mrs. Stern was hiding behind the curtains, watching him, wishing he'd go away. He stared at the windows. They stared back. He decided to try the back door. Maybe Mrs. Stern was deaf. She was old. Old people were often hard of hearing. If she was in the kitchen, she might not have heard his knock.

He pressed his face against the kitchen window, shading his eyes against the glass to get a better look. The room was neat and tidy. There were no dirty dishes in the sink, no pots on top of the stove. A newspaper was spread out on the table as if someone had been reading it there. A bunch of flowers nodded at him in a friendly fashion. Guy breathed a circle on the windowpane and wrote GUY in big letters.

He sat down on the back steps to think. Maybe Mrs. Stern had just nipped down to the corner on an errand and she'd be back any moment. He picked up a handful of pebbles and tossed them in the air one by one.

Minutes passed. Isabelle had told him Mrs. Stern sometimes climbed up on her roof to clean out the gutters.

"At her age!" Isabelle had said admiringly.

The roof was empty today except for a cluster of starlings roosting on the TV antenna, chatting nervously among themselves, passing the time of day.

Then Guy heard someone coming, someone whistling gaily. He hid in the bushes under Mrs. Stern's front windows. If it was Isabelle, he'd pounce out on her and scare her. He hoped it was Isabelle.

It was Philip, delivering his papers. Guy was scared of Philip. Isabelle said Philip was always doing bad things to her, socking her in the stomach, calling her names, stealing her candy. He crouched low, spying on Philip.

Two girls appeared. They stood at the yard's edge talking, watching from the corners of their eyes as Philip folded his newspapers in the special, intricate way he had. Philip frowned and twitched and carried on, Guy thought, like a mad scientist about to blow up the world. The girls acted as if they didn't know he was there. They whispered behind their hands and waited for Philip to notice them.

A caterpillar crawled slowly up Guy's leg, under his jeans, looking for something to eat, maybe. Guy dug his hands in and moved his fingers, looking for the caterpillar so he could pull it out and hurl it onto the grass.

Guy heard a thump nearby. Philip had thrown Mrs. Stern's paper. It had landed right on target, on the stoop. Still whistling, Philip got on his bike and prepared to ride away.

"Oh, hi," he said to the girls, noticing them for the first time.

The girls, looking a little frayed around the edges from all their efforts, said, "Oh, hi!" back.

With fanfare befitting a high-powered motorcycle, Philip took off in a cloud of dust. The girls watched him go. Then they too went on their way. The street was quiet.

Reluctantly, Guy crawled out of his hiding place. He pulled up his jeans to see if the caterpillar had left any marks on him.

He'd come back later, Guy told himself. He was disappointed about not seeing Mrs. Stern. It had been an adventure, coming to her house by himself. But now his adventure was over.

Chapter Nineteen

Guy skipped his way down Mrs. Stern's street and, wouldn't you know, soon came upon a vast clump of violets, growing wild. They were fragrant and delicate, colored white and purple. He picked all his hands could hold. Tomorrow he'd return and pick more.

"Well, hello dere." The large boy, larger even than Philip, loomed in Guy's path, blocking the way. He had slick, dark hair and an earring in one ear. He smiled and his eyes almost disappeared. His gums came down low over his teeth.

"Hello." Guy sidestepped him, not eager to make friends.

"Come on." The boy reached out his hand and took Guy's. "I want to show you something."

Guy knew he shouldn't go with strangers. His mother had told him that and he'd seen movies in school. He sidestepped in the other direction and said, "I have to go home."

The boy kept smiling and pushed back his greasy hair. "It won't take a sec, I promise. I've got something to show you, something you're gonna like."

He laid his arm around Guy's shoulders and steered him toward whatever it was he had to show.

Guy looked nervously over his shoulder. There was no one in sight, no one who would hear him if he cried "Help!" But it was broad daylight. Nothing could happen. He was safe.

There were two others, three in all. One had a mustache that looked like a little mouse lying asleep on his lip. The other one wore a black leather jacket with MONSTER written on the pocket.

Monster is right, Guy thought. And he longed for Isabelle. She'd know what to do. She'd fix their wagon.

The one with the gums said, "It won't take a sec, I promise."

"You already promised once," Guy said.

"Little wise guy, ain't ya?" Fingers tightened on Guy's neck. He pulled away. The fingers followed.

They were grouped around something Guy couldn't see.

"Looka that! Looka the little bugger!" cried the one with the mouse mustache. Guy heard a noise. It didn't sound like any noise he'd heard before. He thought maybe it was an animal caught in a trap. The sound the animal made sent chills up and down his spine.

The group shifted and Guy looked and saw what it was that had made the terrible sound. It was his dog. At least, he thought it was his dog. A tin can weighted down the feather duster tail. The eager amber eyes were dull. But Guy was sure he saw the tail wag feebly as the dog looked up at him. It must be hard to wag a tail with a tin can tied to it, Guy thought. He put out his hand. The dog tried to get to its feet and was shoved roughly back down.

The dog lay still, its sides going in and out, in and out. It was breathing. It was alive.

The boy with MONSTER written on his pocket lit a cigarette and held it dangerously close to the dog's matted fur. The smell of burning filled the air.

Guy couldn't help himself. "Don't," he said, knowing it was a mistake. "Don't hurt him."

The cigarette touched the dog's fur again, and this time the dog howled.

"Gutsy little bugger, ain't he?" Did they mean the dog or did they mean Guy? Hard to tell.

Once again the dog thrashed on the ground, trying to get up. Guy bent down to help him. His hand was kicked away. Suddenly, it was cold. The sun had gone.

"You like dogs, huh, kid? Little kid like you oughta have a dog of his own, right? You want this one? He's got no place to go. You want to buy him?" Their mouths stretched tight in joyless laughter.

"Yes," Guy said. "I'd like him."

"Well, whaddya know? The kid wants to buy our dog. How about that?" They widened their eyes at each other. "How much do you think this here dog's worth? A lotta bread, right? A whole lotta bread."

"I can get some money." The dog watched Guy. It tried once more to rise and got pushed down with the sharp point of a big stick one of them held. This time the dog closed its eyes and lay still.

"I'll go home and get some money," Guy said, through trembling lips. He tried to hold his mouth stiff so they wouldn't see he was afraid. He must be brave. If only Isabelle were here, she'd punch them all out, she'd holler and shout and run. Or someone would come.

"My father has some money."

They exchanged sly glances. "I don't know," MONSTER said. "This here is a very valuable dog. Worth a whole lotta bread, right?" The others nodded, their faces long, their eyes glittering. "I doubt your old man has that kinda bread. This here dog has his papers and all." At this, they went into gales of laughter, shouting, doubling over, thumping each other. "Papers!" they shouted gleefully.

Guy took a couple of secret steps backwards, toward the street. "How much?" he said. "Tell me how much and I'll get it."

The one with the gums said, suddenly calm, "A thousand."

"I'd say more like two." They all had ceased to smile. Their eyes were small and hostile.

"Maybe we better have a conference," the mustached one said, biting his fingernails.

"Yeah," the other two agreed. "But first, we better tie him up so's he don't get lost," the one with the gums said.

Tie who up? Him? Or the dog? Or both?

The rope was as thick as Guy's wrist. They meant him.

"Let's take him back in the woods and tie him to a tree," MONSTER said. "That way, we're sure he don't get loose."

They began to argue about where he should be tied up. When that was settled, they argued about who would do the tying. Their voices rose. They forgot everything else—Guy, the dog, everything. The stick was within reach, Guy realized. He put out his arm, remembering the girl on television, smaller than he, who had broken a bare board with her hands. This stick was his weapon, his only one.

"What is this? Will you looka the little tiger!" In a body, argument forgotten, they came at him. Guy swung the stick and landed a lucky, finger-tingling blow on the side of MONSTER's face. A string of swear words came from MONSTER's throat and he fell to one knee. Crouching, circling, the other two came at Guy, one to the right, the other to the left. In a panic, Guy kept swinging, not knowing what else to do. Once the stick stopped moving, he'd had it.

Thunk! He felt a terrible sharp pain. Something had hit him on the back of his head. He let out a yelp of pain, heard someone say, "What'd ya have to go and do that for?" and another voice said "Cops!" and that was all. That was the last he remembered.

Chapter Twenty

"Lucky the kid has a lot of hair."

Guy opened his eyes. His head hurt. Eyes as blue and shiny as two marbles stared down into his.

"You all right, kid?" The policeman held out a cup of water and Guy drank some. His head felt like a balloon with too much air in it—swollen, light, ready to take off and fly high.

A second policeman knelt to inspect the back of Guy's head. "Three to one and them big as any man, and they bean the kid with a rock." He shook his head.

Guy sat up.

"Where's the dog?" he said.

"In the car. He's a little shook up, you might say, but he'll be fine. He's only a pup. Is he yours?"

Guy shook his head. Something seemed to be loose in it.

"No," he said. "I wish he was."

"Try standing, son." The blue-eyed policeman helped Guy to his feet. "Anything broken?" He ran an expert hand over Guy to see if he was in one piece. "Can you walk?"

"Sure." Guy tottered a few steps. He felt like lying down again. Most of all, he wanted to go home.

"We'll run you home now," the other policeman said, as if he'd read Guy's mind. "Just check in so's your folks won't worry. Imagine they're already worried, you not home and it suppertime already."

Guy looked at the police car parked at the curb.

"Am I going home in that?" he said.

"What else? Hop in."

Guy smiled. He was going home in a police car.

"We'll drop you off, then run the pooch over to the Humane Society," the policeman said. "They'll fix him up good as new."

The dog lay on the back seat. Its eyes were closed. Its sides were moving as it breathed slowly, in and out. Guy got in the front seat, sandwiched between the two policemen.

"Where to, chief?"

Guy looked up at them. They meant him.

"Twenty-two Hot Water Street," he said. The car pulled out. They were on the way.

"Hot Water Street, huh?" the blue-eyed cop grinned. "They'll think you're in hot water for sure when they see you coming home in this."

Guy's heart hammered. That's what he hoped.

"Excuse me, sir, but do you think you could make your light go?"

"Sure thing. I can even turn on the siren, if you want."

Guy thought that over. "No thanks, just the light would be neat."

The patrol car turned into Hot Water Street. Guy closed his eyes tight. Oh Lord, please let them see me, he prayed. Let Becca see me. Please let a bunch of kids be hanging around. Let them all see me. Please, Lord. I won't ask for anything else if you'll just let that happen.

The Lord must've heard. Three boys whizzed by on bikes, then turned to stare as the police car slowed, blue lights flashing.

"Which house is yours?" the blue-eyed cop said.

"That one," Guy pointed. He saw Becca in the front yard. She and a friend were playing fairy princess. Becca had just made a deep curtsey when the car pulled up and came to a stop.

"Not just a little siren?" the policeman asked again. "Just to make 'em sit up and take notice?"

"Well, okay," Guy said. "But only a little."

The cop flicked a switch. The siren sounded very loud to Guy. Becca froze. Her friend clapped her hands over her ears and ran behind the big maple tree. The three boys on bikes stood on the sidewalk across from Guy's house, waiting.

First the driver got out. Then the other policeman. Then came Guy.

Becca's hand flew toward her mouth. Then she ran to the house, screaming, "It's Guy! It's Guy! The policeman brought Guy home!"

Becca had some loud voice. Guy had never realized how loud it was until now. He smiled, listening to her.

Across the street the three kids on bikes watched, their mouths hanging open. Up and down the block people came out and stood watching. It wasn't every day a police car, lights flashing, siren sounding, delivered someone to his front door on Hot Water Street.

"What's going on here?" Guy's father came to the door, glasses pushed up on his forehead, newspaper in his hand.

"Your boy got into some trouble, sir," the blue-eyed policeman said.

"My boy never gets into trouble," Guy's father said firmly. "He's a good boy. A very good boy. Never caused his mother or me a speck of trouble."

"He is a good boy," the policeman agreed. "And a brave one, too." Then he told what had happened to Guy. And the dog. By this time Guy's mother and grandmother were gathered around, listening. Guy's mother insisted on inspecting his head and then called the doctor to make an appointment to bring Guy to see him. The cut on Guy's head had stopped bleeding; it wasn't even very deep.

"Like I said, it's good your boy has such a fine head of hair," the policeman said. "Acted as padding when they walloped him." Then he took out his notebook and wrote down everything Guy could remember about the MONSTER, the one with the gums, and the one with the mouse mustache. That's the way Guy thought of it, the mouse mustache.

"All right, that's everything, then." The policeman put away his notebook. "We're going to run the pooch over to the Humane Society, see what they can find." He tipped his hat to the crowd. "I'll be in touch."

For the first time, Guy's grandmother spoke.

"What will happen to the dog?" she said.

The cop shrugged. "Hard to say. Dog's got no license, no identification tags of any kind. Probably a stray. Chances are they'll put it up for adoption. If no one claims it after a certain length of time, well . . ." The cop shrugged again.

Guy's grandmother, dark eyes gleaming, looked hard at Guy.

"I want that dog," he heard himself say. "It's like the dog I wanted all along. I think it's the one I wanted. It's a really nice dog. Just the right size. I bet he'd never make a mess or chew things or anything. He'd be a good watchdog too." Guy looked up at his mother and father.

"Well." Guy's father cleared his throat. "I guess that could be arranged. Thank you, officer. We'll call the Humane Society within the next few days, see how things stand."

The policemen tipped their hats.

"Good luck, son," the blue-eyed one said to Guy. By this time, quite a crowd had gathered, wondering what was going on. The policemen got back into their car and, lights flashing, drove away.

"Come in, Guy, let me have a good look at you," Guy's mother said. As he turned to go in, he heard Becca say in her loud voice, "Oh, it's my brother. He got into trouble and the police had to bring him home. His name is Guy. Yes, he's my brother. He's eight. Yes, his name is Guy. He's eight. He got into trouble. Yes, he's . . ."

Guy smiled. If Becca had anything to do with it, everyone in town would know who Guy Gibbs was.

Chapter Twenty-one

"*So there I am, my father's driving me to school, and* all of a sudden the radio announcer says, 'An eight-year-old boy fought off three hoodlums yesterday in an effort to rescue a stray dog the hoodlums were holding captive. The boy, Guy Gibbs of Hot Water Street, told police the dog was being tortured by the three and he . . .' blah, blah, blah," said Isabelle, filling in for what she couldn't remember.

"So I said, 'That's Guy!' and my father says, 'Unh huh,' the way he does when he's not really listening.

When I got to school I told Mrs. Esposito and she said I could run down to Guy's room and check. His teacher said he'd be in later, that his mother called and she was taking him to the doctor. You don't think there could be two eight-year-old boys both named Guy Gibbs living on Hot Water Street, do you?" Isabelle said.

"I doubt it," Jane Malone answered. "Probably his mother had to take him to the doctor because he lost a lot of blood."

"Guy lost a lot of blood? My gosh, I can't believe it. That little weasel. Why wasn't I along? If I was there, I could've pinned their ears back. I could've helped Guy. I miss all the good things. Boy, they'll never call him a goody-goody again." Isabelle's eyes widened and she clutched Jane's arm. "You don't think Guy's gonna die or anything, do you?"

"Of course not," Jane said in her practical way. "I like that word 'hoodlum.' Hoodlum. It sounds just like what it is. Hoodlum." Jane was getting carried away by the word. Jane was a word person, always trying out new words.

"Isabelle," Jane said, "can you come—"

But Isabelle was distracted by the sight of Herbie, staggering under a load of books and papers. "Hey, Herb!" she hollered. Jane flinched and stuck a finger in each ear. "You hear about Guy getting rescued by the cops yesterday?"

"Guy?" Herbie said vaguely. As if he'd never heard

of Guy. "What happened? Did they have a shoot-out?"

Isabelle stopped moving. Hands, eyes, legs, arms, feet, all came to a dead halt. "A shoot-out?" she said. "My gosh, maybe they did. Maybe that's why Guy lost so much blood."

"He lost blood?" Now she had Herbie's full attention. "Maybe we oughta go down to the hospital and offer to give him blood. You know what your blood type is? Maybe it won't match Guy's. Maybe mine will."

Herbie screwed up his face. "I never gave blood. I'm scared it might hurt. How much blood did Guy lose?"

"Hey, slow down, Herb," Isabelle urged. "He's gonna be all right. He's at the doctor's now, but he'll be in school later on. You wanna fight at my house today?"

"I can't," Herbie said. "Got too much to do. My assistant editor is coming over after school. We gotta make plans. He—"

"Your assistant editor!" Isabelle's voice rang out. People turned to stare. "Your assistant editor!" she screeched. "I thought *I* was your assistant editor! What goes on?"

Herbie looked embarrassed. "Well, Chauncey called up and said he would be my assistant editor on account of he voted me into the job in the first place. So I said okay. So Chauncey's my assistant editor." Herbie looked at the floor, not willing to meet Isabelle's indignant gaze.

"Well, all right for you. That's the last time I offer to help you, Herbie. Fine pal you are. I said I'd be your right-hand man. All right for you, Herb."

Chauncey came chugging up to Herbie. "Meet me outside right after the bell goes," Chauncey directed, looking at his watch. "We have a tight schedule. I'm trying to line up a photographer. It's not gonna be easy, though. Remember"—again Chauncey checked his watch—"right after the bell rings. Outside." Chauncey chugged away.

"Boy, you got your work cut out for you, Herb. I'll say that. I bet you'll wind up in the booby hatch with that guy on your side."

"You're just jealous, Isabelle," Herbie said with dignity. "You're jealous because you're not the assistant editor."

"That's what you think!" Isabelle cried. "Next time you want somebody to fight with, try fighting with your assistant editor. That oughta be a barrel of laughs. Don't forget who your friends were before you were somebody. That's all I've got to say. Just don't forget who your friends were before you turned famous."

"Isabelle, can you come—" Jane Malone said. And stopped talking.

"Can I come where?" Isabelle demanded.

Jane looked around. "Are you listening to me?" she asked.

"Sure," said Isabelle.

"Well, my mother said I could ask a friend to come

to stay at my house for dinner and the night on Saturday," Jane said. "And I picked you. My father might take us to the movies and to McDonald's after. Can you?"

Isabelle was stunned. Never before had she been asked to Jane's house. "Can I!" she cried. "I would very much love to come to your house, Jane."

"That's good." Jane smiled. "Ask your mother when you go home today, all right? Then call me up and tell me."

"Sure." Isabelle punched Jane gently on the arm. "Sure," she said again, smiling at Jane.

I didn't even know she liked me that much, Isabelle thought. Jane is my best friend.

The thought warmed her.

Chapter Twenty-two

"Tell me what happened right from the beginning," Isabelle directed.

"Well, first, I went to Mrs. Stern's house and she wasn't home, so I hid in the bushes and watched when Philip delivered the paper and then—"

"I don't mean that beginning," Isabelle said impatiently. "I mean when the hoodlums got you. Start there."

So Guy told her about picking the violets and about the one saying "Hello, dere" to him and not letting go of him. About MONSTER and the other two. About the cigarette and the smell of burning and the tin can tied to the dog's tail.

"Then they said they were gonna tie me up while they planned how much money they wanted for the dog," Guy said. "And I thought about you and what you'd do, and so I started swinging the big stick, which was the only weapon I could find, and then they knocked me out."

"Why didn't you wait for me?" Isabelle wailed. "Oh, why didn't you!" She had missed the biggest excitement she might ever know.

"I did," Guy said simply. "You said you were real busy when I asked you if you'd thought of anything. But I waited anyway. When you didn't come, I decided to go to Mrs. Stern's by myself. To ask her about the paint."

He was right. She had said that.

"Guy," she said. "You know what?"

"No. What?"

"You did it yourself," she said. "You kept asking and asking if I'd think of a way to make them stop teasing you, calling you all those names and everything. And you did it all by yourself. Don't you see?"

A smile broke across Guy's face slowly. "You're right," he said. "I did."

"Excellent. Excellent," Isabelle told him, holding up the index finger on each hand and jitterbugging around him in a complete circle.

"Hi, Guy. You wanna come over my house after school? My cat had two more kittens. You can come see 'em if you want."

"Hello, Bernie. She did! Neat-o. Sure, I'll come."

"What's that on the back of your head?" Bernie asked. "You cut yourself?"

Guy looked at Isabelle. "I was in an accident," he said.

"That's my friend Bernie," Guy said. "He's in my class. His cat had kittens while he was eating a piece of toast in the kitchen."

"Jane Malone asked me to come stay overnight Saturday. We're going to the movies and to McDonald's after," Isabelle said.

"What're you gonna have at McDonald's?" Guy asked.

"I don't know."

"I always plan what I'm gonna have ahead of time," Guy confided. "If I don't, I get too confused when the girl asks me and I always pick something I don't like. So I write down what I want on a little piece of paper, and that way I know exactly what I'm gonna get."

"That's not a bad idea," Isabelle said.

"They said I could keep the dog," Guy told Isabelle. "He doesn't have a license or anything. They said if nobody owned it, I could keep it."

"Terrific. What're you gonna call it?" Isabelle said.

"Jake," said Guy, looking at her, eyes glistening. 'I'm calling it Jake."

"What if it's a girl?"

"If it's a girl," Guy said slowly, "I'm calling it Isabelle. I already decided."

"Isabelle?"

"Sure. It even sort of looks like you," Guy said.

"Cool," said Isabelle, without enthusiasm.

"Sure. It's got brown eyes and brown hair, like you."

"Yeah, but you hafta think about when it's out at night and you're trying to get it to come in. So you're out there, calling, 'Here, Isabelle! Come on in, Isabelle!' I don't think that sounds too hot." She'd been told she looked like lots of things, but never, not even by Philip, had she been told she looked like a dog.

"Besides, if you call it Isabelle," Isabelle said, trying to talk Guy out of it, "it'd sound silly. 'Here, Isabelle' "—she imitated Guy calling his dog—" 'Good boy, Isabelle! Supper's ready! Come inside, Isabelle, before your tootsies get all wet.'

"How would that sound?" Isabelle asked indignantly.

"So? I don't think there's anything bad about that," Guy said.

"What's bad is, you would sound exactly like my mother. That's what's bad."

"So what if I sound like your mother." There was something he'd forgotten, something important he'd left out.

"I know!" Guy remembered what it was. "You know how I got home? After they bonked me on the head?"

"No. How'd you get home?"

"In a police car," Guy said, in hushed tones.

Isabelle narrowed her eyes at him and scratched herself, knowing what was coming, pretending she didn't care.

"With the lights flashing?" she said, leaning down to pull up her socks so he couldn't see her face.

"Yup."

"How about the siren?" she asked, inspecting a hole in the toe of her Adidas.

Guy only nodded.

"I can't stand it," Isabelle said, clapping a hand to her head. "I cannot stand it!"

"I know." Guy couldn't help grinning. "And you know something else?"

She shook her head.

"I'm gonna be on the six o'clock news. Tonight."

Mary Eliza Shook came hurtling by at that moment.

"How's your little brudder?" she said sarcastically. Mary Eliza was always the last to get the word.

"Watch the six o'clock news tonight and find out," Isabelle said.

No actress ever had a better exit line. Mary Eliza stood there gawking at them.

"The six o'clock news?" she finally squeaked.

"Yeah, you can't miss it," Isabelle said, smiling sweetly. "It comes on at six o'clock."

There were so many good things about Guy's adventure and its aftermath that Isabelle couldn't pick her favorite. But certainly one of her favorites was telling Philip about Guy being on the six o'clock news.

"You're putting me on," he said scornfully when she told him. "Not that little squirt. I don't believe you."

She shrugged, knowing that for once she had the upper hand. "Okay, don't," she said. "See if I care."

And, although the rule was no television on school nights, Isabelle's mother made an exception.

At two minutes to six, the family gathered in front of the TV set. "It's Channel Eight," Isabelle said. Philip just looked at her. He was the official dial twirler.

"Good evening, ladies and gentlemen. Channel Eight here." The anchorman had a silly face, Isabelle thought. He laughed too much, too. The first story was about a suspicious fire set in a downtown hotel. The second story was about a group of concerned citizens picketing a proposed motel in the next town.

"If he's gonna be on, why don't they put him on?" Philip groused.

"If you don't wanta watch, don't." Isabelle sat on the floor and waited.

"Now for the last story, last but certainly not least," the anchorman said. "An eight-year-old boy became a hero yesterday when he stood off the attacks of three hoodlums who captured him and held him hostage against the release of a stray dog the hoodlums offered

134

to sell to the boy for a thousand dollars."

The camera zoomed in and Guy stood there in his own front yard. He didn't smile but looked straight at the camera.

"Guy Gibbs," the person holding the microphone said, "how did you have the courage to do what you did?" The microphone waited for Guy to speak.

He opened his mouth, then closed it.

"The kid's lost his voice," Philip said.

Isabelle clutched herself around the middle with both arms, rocking back and forth, willing Guy to speak.

He cleared his throat as the camera ground away.

"It was Isabelle," he said, in a loud, clear voice. "My friend Isabelle."

"Isabelle?" the interviewer asked animatedly.

"She's my friend and she learned me, I mean, taught me how to stand up to things. So when they came at me, I tried to figure what Isabelle would do. And I did it." Guy's mouth clamped shut.

Isabelle's mother laid a hand on her arm, gently. Philip said, "Sheesh!" but that was all.

The camera zoomed in on a shot of Guy holding his dog.

"Just thirty seconds left now," the anchorman said jovially. "Tell us what your dog's name is, Guy Gibbs."

"Isabelle," said Guy. "I was going to call it Jake, but we found out he was a girl. So I'm calling it Isabelle."

A commercial about breakfast cereal came on. In Isabelle's living room there was silence.

"Well, that certainly is quite a testimonial," Isabelle's mother said at last, in a little choked-up voice.

"Not too many guys I know have a sister who gets a dog named after her," Philip said. The telephone rang. Isabelle ran to answer it. It was Aunt Maude.

"The strangest thing just happened," Aunt Maude said. "I was watching the six o'clock news and a little boy who looked familiar was on. He was getting some sort of award, don't you know, and he said his dog was named Isabelle. Was that the little boy who comes over every Sunday to fight or was that the little boy who said I looked like his uncle? It was one or the other. The strangest coincidence, isn't it? There he was on the television. He looked a little peaked, too. I really think his mother should've kept him in bed."

Aunt Maude sneezed three times: choo, choo, choo. Isabelle thought she sounded like a kitten sneezing.

"I must be coming down with something," Aunt Maude said. "Probably the same thing the little boy had. I couldn't make head or tail of it but just thought I'd call to let you know he was on the six o'clock news. Tell your mother I'll stop by after church on Sunday. I've got a new hat I want to show her. Good night, dear." And Aunt Maude hung up.

Chapter Twenty-three

"Well, I'm off." Guy's grandmother announced, suitcase in hand.

"I thought you were staying longer," Guy said.

"I've been here long enough. Time to go. Your room looks nice, Guy. I like the color."

"Mrs. Stern helped me mix it. How do you like the stars?"

"They're lovely. Look real."

"I'm sleeping out in a tent at my friend Bernie's house," Guy said. "He said I could borrow his brother's sleeping bag. His mother leaves the back door open in case Bernie gets scared." He looked at his grandmother. "Sometimes Bernie says he gets scared if a big animal comes along in the night and makes noises. Or if it starts to lightning and thunder. That's why his mother leaves the door open—so's he can get back in."

"That'll be fun," Guy's grandmother said.

"I told Mrs. Stern about you," Guy said. "I thought maybe you and her could be friends."

"That's nice, Guy. Maybe next time I come I'll meet Mrs. Stern. I'd like that."

A taxi beeped outside.

Guy's grandmother put out her arms. "How about a hug before I take off?" she said.

"Okay." He put down his books. "I'll miss you," he said. He put his arms around her and kissed her cheek.

"Well," she said, smiling, "that's better. Hugs are for everybody. Kisses you save for somebody special." She set her hat straight on her head.

"Give my regards to the paper boy," she said. And, "Good-bye, Isabelle," she said to the dog. Guy watched her go down the path and get into the taxi. Then he got down on the floor and rested his head alongside the dog's.

"I might call you Jake, after all," Guy said. Isabelle licked his face. "You look more like a Jake. Jake's a better name for a dog, anyway. Right, Jake?" Isabelle wagged her tail in agreement.